Nothing Rhymes with Justice

JAMES A. BOOKER

Portland • Oregon
INKWATERPRESS.COM

Copyright © 2009 by James A. Booker

Cover Photo by Enge, istockphoto
Front Cover design by David Aragon
Cover layout and interior design by Masha Shubin

This is a work of fiction. The events described here are imaginary. The settings and characters are fictitious or used in a fictitious manner and do not represent specific places or living or dead people. Any resemblance is entirely coincidental.

All rights reserved. No part of this book may be reproduced or transmitted in any form or by any means whatsoever, including photocopying, recording or by any information storage and retrieval system, without written permission from the publisher and/or author. Contact Inkwater Press at 6750 SW Franklin Street, Suite A, Portland, OR 97223-2542. 503.968.6777

www.inkwaterpress.com

ISBN-13 978-1-59299-410-6
ISBN-10 1-59299-410-5

Publisher: Inkwater Press

Printed in the U.S.A.
All paper is acid free and meets all ANSI standards for archival quality paper.

Sing a song of virtues,
Aesthetics and the rest,
Poetics is a problem
When labeling the best.
Beauty rhymes with duty,
Ideal rhymes with real.
Love with dove and good with could,
But nothing rhymes with justice.
Distributive, retributive,
Jury, hurry, furry,
Even fudge will rhyme with judge,
But nothing rhymes with justice.

*With appreciation to my proof-reader and technical advisor,
Paulette, who also happens to be my wife,
and to David Aragon, the talented graphic
artist who designed the cover.*

PART I

1975

1

The Chicago evening rush-hour traffic was beginning to thin out as Wagner left the interstate. He turned onto Highway 38 and headed west. The tempo of the traffic decreased considerably as soon as he left the busy four-lane highway, and he relaxed a little. It occurred to him that he had been driving for half an hour without turning on the radio. That was quite unusual for him. Ordinarily the radio got just about as much wear as the carburetor. He turned it on, but hardly noticed what was playing.

In the rear view mirror he caught sight of a sign marking the Chicago city limits. It read: "Welcome to Chicago. Richard J. Daley, Mayor." It seemed to Wagner as if Richard J. Daley had been mayor of Chicago just about forever.

Then came the suburbs. Without a sign, there would have been no indication that one was leaving Chicago. "Commuterland," he thought as he drove through one suburban community after another: Elmhurst, Villa Park, Lombard, Glen Ellyn, Wheaton, Winfield. He knew that many of the local inhabitants worked in Chicago and spent two or three hours a day traveling back and forth between home and job.

"I wonder how many of these people live out here because they're afraid to raise their families in the city," he pondered, not for the first time. "Well, at least they have jobs to go to."

Wagner was vaguely aware of signs indicating the distance to West Chicago and the National Accelerator Laboratory, but he ignored them. His destination was several miles past the western suburbs. Besides, he had other things on his mind.

He drove past the government lab and picked up signs for Geneva. Judge Carrol lived near Geneva. Wagner was going to a Geneva conference. Not quite, at least in the traditional sense. It was the wrong Geneva, and Wagner was hardly a diplomat.

"Why would the judge want to talk to me in person?" he asked himself for the umpteenth time. The phone call had hinted at the possibility of a job, but that seemed highly unlikely. What kind of a job could a retired federal judge have to offer him? It had to have some connection with that recent fracas in court. How else would the judge have heard about Wagner? He hadn't done anything else recently to attract much attention.

Wagner reached his destination just a few minutes before the designated time. He started to congratulate himself for having estimated the driving time so accurately, but then felt a twinge of embarrassment over such a foolish notion. After all, he was familiar enough with the entire Chicago area to know just about how long it would take to reach any part of it, barring some unforeseen event.

The judge's house was large, probably sixty or seventy years old, and was located on a lot which was at least two acres in size. The yard was neatly maintained, but the house was overdue for a coat of paint. The car parked next to the house was a four-year-old Buick. Wagner pulled up behind it. He turned off the engine and waited a few minutes in order to avoid arriving early. At one minute before the hour, he went to the door and rang the bell. It annoyed him that he felt somewhat nervous.

The man who answered the door was about seventy years old. Wagner recognized Judge Carrol from pictures in the newspaper, but he had never met him.

"Good evening, Mr. Wagner," said the older man. "Please come in."

"Thank you, sir," replied Wagner, trying hard to look poised despite his sense of insecurity.

"Let me take your coat. May I offer you a drink?"

"Please," Wagner answered, although he didn't especially want one.

"What would you like?"

"Bourbon and water would be fine," said Wagner, somewhat surprised by the judge's friendliness and hospitality.

"I have some excellent scotch."

"Thanks, but I've never cultivated a taste for scotch."

"Very well, then. Bourbon and water it is."

Wagner looked around the spacious living room while the judge performed the bartending functions. The furniture was elegant, but it appeared to be at least fifty years old. Apparently there was no one else in the house.

"Here you are," said the judge as he handed Wagner a large glass. Wagner accepted it, expressed his appreciation, and took a sip while the judge sat down in a chair opposite him.

"Do you have any idea why I've asked you to come here?"

"Not for sure. You weren't very specific on the phone."

"But you must have some notion or you wouldn't have come."

Wagner was mildly irritated by this cat-and-mouse approach, but he simply said, "I presume that it has something to do with my losing my job. I can't think of anything else I've done recently that would have caught your attention." He felt his palms start to sweat and automatically cooled them on the glass.

"You're right, of course. I'd like to hear your side of the story. Before we continue any further, however, let me say that anything you tell me will be held in strictest confidence. Conversely, I expect the same from you. If you disclose to anyone the nature of this visit, I shall deny that I ever saw you. Do we understand each other?" He leaned back in his chair, apparently comfortable with his superior role.

"No problem here," said Wagner. He then took a long drink in an effort to conceal his mounting curiosity. Somehow he found it difficult to act casual in the judge's presence.

The judge continued. "As I understand it, you struck a defendant who had just been acquitted in a court of law. Would you care to explain your action?"

Wagner's knuckles turned white as he gripped the glass. It took him a minute to compose his thoughts. Finally he spoke.

"I was working with the vice squad over on the South Side. As you must know, prostitution is so rampant over there that nobody can do much about it, but we were trying to put one particular operator out of action. His name is Roosevelt Rose—'Rosie' to just about everybody. My partner and I spent nearly a month watching his operation. He had about twenty girls working for him. He was so sure that nobody could touch him that he flaunted his act. He deliberately played the part of the stereotypical black pimp—drove a gaudy Cadillac, wore a Panama hat, the whole bit. He even wore a rose in his lapel as a sort of trademark. But there was nothing rosy about him. He'd beat his girls if they didn't make enough money for him. He was known to recruit girls as young as fourteen and get them hooked on heroin so they'd have to stay with him. He's a real sweet customer.

"Well, we finally got enough evidence against him and made the arrest. He practically laughed in our faces when we arrested him. His lawyer posted bail an hour later and got him released, but he showed up for trial. He knew he had nothing to worry about. We were counting on two of his veteran hookers to testify against him, but they disappeared, and the judge threw our case out for lack of evidence." Wagner set his glass down and squirmed uncomfortably.

"As Rose walked by me, he stopped, stuck a wooden match in his mouth, grinned, and gave me the finger. That was more than I could take. I jumped up and hit him. Smashed his nose. He had to be taken to the hospital. His lawyer made some kind of a deal not to sue the city and me for battery if the department would pull my badge. So that's what they did. Now Rosie is back in business, and I'm out of a job."

The judge was silent for a moment as he reflected on Wagner's account. Finally he spoke in slow, measured tones.

"What do you think should be done about all this?" he asked.

The question caught Wagner by surprise.

"What's there to be done? The case was thrown out of court, and I have no more official status. I doubt if even you could get a new trial."

"Ah, yes. You have a degree in criminal justice and therefore understand the finer points of our judicial system." There was a tinge of irony in the judge's voice.

"So what options are left?" Wagner asked.

Again the judge spoke in that slow, deliberate manner which he must have cultivated during a lifetime of legal practice.

"Mr. Rose is out there bragging about how he outwitted the system. Of course, he didn't do any such thing, but he had enough money to hire someone who knew the rules of the game. Legally, our hands are tied."

"So it seems," Wagner agreed.

""But just let your imagination roam a little. For instance, what do you suppose would happen to our friend's image if he were to find that nice purple Cadillac pressed into a compact cube?"

Wagner just stared for a minute. "You've got to be kidding," he said. At the same time, he made a mental note of the fact that the judge knew the color of the car, and he hadn't mentioned it.

The judge shrugged casually. "Tomorrow you can go and look for yourself."

Wagner was suddenly aware of two conflicting feelings, one of disbelief and the other of immense satisfaction.

"But a trick like that would hardly put Rosie out of business," he replied at last.

"His business will soon put him out of business," quipped the judge. "He has an advanced case of a rather exotic social disease."

Wagner's mind made a rapid calculation of all the information he had just received. Then he said, "You must have quite an organization. You know all about Rosie. You know a lot about me. The only reason you asked me to tell you about my run-in with Rosie was to get my reaction. You already knew the details. And that stunt with the Cadillac would require a tow truck, a scrap metal facility, and a truck with a heavy winch to bring the cubed Caddy back. That's assuming you're not just pulling my leg about all this."

"I didn't invite you here to pull your leg, as you put it. I want you to work for me. I'm going to make you a rather unconventional offer. If you accept it, regular deposits will be made into your checking account with no questions asked. If you decline my offer, I must insist on the confidential treatment of this information. As I have already indicated, if you tell anyone about it, I will deny that I ever spoke to you. Would you like for me to continue?"

Wagner nodded. "I'm too curious not to hear you out."

"Very well, then. Let me refill your glass, and we'll get down to business."

Wagner accepted another bourbon and water. The judge sat down again. He leaned back and looked pensive as he began his monologue.

"I was a member of the legal profession for thirty-eight years. I started as a junior member of a law firm and retired as a federal judge. I devoted my entire professional career to what one might idealistically term the pursuit of justice."

The judge took a sip of his drink and then stared at the coffee table for a moment.

"I don't think you can possibly imagine how disillusioned I felt when I finally had to admit to myself that our system is hopelessly flawed."

It occurred to Wagner that he had heard that observation enough times for it to become somewhat of a cliché, but he remained attentive.

Judge Carrol's facial expression suddenly made him look much older. His poise and dignity were gone. He appeared deflated and dejected. When he spoke again, his voice was much softer.

"The pursuit of justice is one of man's most fundamental drives. Plato began his <u>Republic</u> with a discourse on justice. Countless philosophers, ethicists, theologians and moralists have written about it. I suppose that is because we all have a natural expectation that we should be treated as well as everybody else. But there is a curious dichotomy involved. After all is said and done, we can't even agree on the definition of justice, much less achieve it to any satisfactory degree."

He looked up vaguely, as if he were searching for something on the ceiling.

"Perhaps the best definition available is the Latin *suum quique tribuere*, which is roughly 'rendering unto each one his due.' But just what is each one's due, and who determines it? That's where the rub comes. A judge is supposed to have some special insight into that sort of question. I wonder how many actually do."

He paused for a moment and looked down at the coffee table again. Wagner resisted an urge to glance at his watch.

"As a child, you automatically expect to be treated as well as your siblings. If your brother gets more to eat than you, you become resentful. If you are punished more severely than your sister, you feel abused. The expectation of equal treatment is there right from the start, but this ultimately leads to disappointment. Life seldom treats us that fairly."

Suddenly the judge looked up from the coffee table as if he were abruptly reminded of his surroundings. He took a quick sip of his drink as if by nervous reaction.

"I beg your pardon. I'm getting carried away with theoretical digression. I didn't invite you here to hear me lecture."

"That's quite all right, sir," said Wagner, but he was still wondering what the older man had in mind.

"I won't bore you with all the details of my disenchantment with my chosen profession. Suffice it to say that I found myself on more than one occasion in the same position as the judge who let Rose go free. It probably didn't occur to you that there wasn't much choice involved. I happen to know that the judge didn't like that decision any more than you did."

"No, that possibility really hadn't occurred to me," Wagner admitted.

"It was all in the nature of the system. For so long we were concerned with the rights of the accused that we caused the pendulum to swing away from the rights of the community at large. That's why we find people like your Mr. Rose getting away with all kinds of crimes, and all too often we can't do very much about it."

"I'd say that's a fair generalization, but it still surprises me to hear it from a federal judge."

"Then you'll be even more surprised when you hear what I plan to do about the system, my friend."

"Like putting all the pimpmobiles in Chicago through the trash masher?"

The judge smiled thinly. "Something like that. You see, I have some associates who likewise deplore the inadequacies of our system of criminal justice. Some of these people are willing to help finance certain—projects. Basically, that is how I am able to offer you a respectable salary for your involvement."

Wagner finished his drink before answering.

"Are we talking about pulling a few nuisance stunts, or are we talking vigilante?"

"Maybe a little of both."

Wagner frowned. "I don't know. I've always played it pretty straight."

"Like punching a defendant in a courtroom?"

"That was an exception."

"I'd say it was a rather significant exception. In the first place, it demonstrated your disapproval of the system. In the second place, it not only cost you your job in Chicago, it also greatly diminished your prospects of finding another position elsewhere."

Judge Carrol hesitated for a moment to let the truth of his observations sink in. Then he continued. "If you decide to work with us, I will not try to coerce you into doing anything which goes against your better judgment. Furthermore, if you wish to withdraw from the agreement at any time, I will use my professional influence to help you find suitable employment in another state."

Wagner declined the offer of a refill of his drink while he pondered the strange proposal.

"I'll have to admit, I'm interested. I'd have to know more, though."

"I'd suggest that you inspect Mr. Rose's automobile tomorrow. It will be in the parking place which he reserves for it. I imagine he'll have difficulty moving it from there, though, because it won't roll very well in its new configuration."

"I'll take your word for it. But that's just a clever stunt. You must have something more persuasive than that in mind."

The judge smiled again. "Of course. We'll get to that all in good time."

"OK, let's say I go along with this. How do we operate?"

"You will receive a phone call from someone with a code name. You will not recognize the voice, and you will not be able to trace the call. You will be given your instructions, including how to contact the people who will assist you. You will know only as much as is necessary for the accomplishment of the task. This is for your protection as well as theirs. Obviously, no one can force you to tell what you do not know."

"Are there other ex-cops in your organization?"

"Our associates represent a wide range of vocations and skills," the judge replied vaguely. "They were contacted for the same reason as you. Each of them has expressed strong dissatisfaction with our system of criminal justice. That is the common denominator, so to speak."

"And you say that when I get ready to quit, you'll help me find a job in my line. What kind of a recommendation could you give me?"

"You'll receive credit for doing some undercover work for the Justice Department."

Wagner frowned again. "Is there any truth to that?"

Judge Carrol smiled mysteriously. "What do you think?"

"I think you've answered just about all the questions you're going to."

"You're very perceptive."

"But not very bright. I can't think of any good reason to accept your offer. In fact, I can imagine it getting me into a lot of trouble."

"That possibility does exist for all of us."

"Then why does the idea intrigue me so?"

"I can't imagine."

"How would it be if I give it a try and see how it goes?"

"I believe that possibility is within the terms of my offer."

Wagner stood up and took a deep breath. "All right," he said. "I'll give it a go."

"Excellent," replied the judge as he extended his hand. "I regret that I will not be able to offer you my hospitality while we are associated, but it would not be wise for you to come here again. I shall contact you in a few days for your first assignment. You may expect to be telephoned early in the morning. The code name will be Benjamin."

"What if I need to contact you?"

The judge shook his head. "You will have to wait until I call you. The less each associate knows, the greater the security for all of us. Don't forget that."

Wagner shook his head. "I can't believe I'm standing here listening to all this from a federal judge."

"Perhaps I'll tell you how all this started some day, but this is not the appropriate time."

"I suppose not," Wagner replied for no particular reason.

"I've told you all you need to know for now. I'm very pleased with your decision to join us. I expect you to be a valuable asset to our group. You have a reputation for being quite resourceful."

Wagner shook hands with the judge again, thanked him for the drinks, and left. A light spring rain was falling as he drove back to the city. He turned on the radio, which was habitually tuned to a classical FM station. An orchestra was playing Handel's "Water Music."

"I suppose that's as appropriate as anything," he thought.

By the time he reached the Chicago city limits, the whole visit seemed like a dream.

"I guess I'll have to drive over to the South Side tomorrow and check out Rosie's Cadillac after all," he decided. Somehow, he didn't doubt what he would find there.

2

At about ten the next morning, Wagner reached the apartment building on the South Side where Rose lived. Actually he owned the entire building, but he used most of it to operate his "business." Wagner and his partner, Fletcher, had spent many cold nights watching people enter and leave the building. In fact, Wagner couldn't remember if he had ever seen the building in the daylight.

As he approached the parking lot adjacent to the building, Wagner could see a crowd of Blacks around Rosie's reserved parking place. Against his better judgment, Wagner got out of his car and walked closer to the spot. As he neared the group, one of the men recognized him and said something. A man in a green silk suit turned and glared at Wagner. It was Rose himself. As some of the people moved to one side, Wagner could see that the fancy purple Cadillac was now a tightly compressed cube.

"Looks like you had a little accident," Wagner commented casually. "That sure is a shame. Nice car like that."

"I know you did this, Wagner," replied the man in the green suit. "Ain't nobody else that would mess with me like that. I'm gonna get your ass one of these days."

"I doubt it," Wagner countered. "Fletcher wouldn't like that. Besides, you don't really think I did this. If I had, you'd be inside that car."

The pimp glanced at the mangled wreckage, then scowled back at Wagner. "You'd best get out of here while you can.

And don't come back. You lost your badge. You got no more business here."

Wagner smiled humorlessly and strolled back to his own car, willing to concede the last word to his adversary.

◆ ❖ ◆

He didn't have to wait long for his first contact from his new employer. His telephone rang at 6:30 the next morning, just two days after his conversation with Judge Carrol.

"Good morning, Mr. Wagner. This is Benjamin," said a strange voice which did not sound at all like that of the judge.

"Let me find a pencil—OK, go ahead," muttered Wagner through a sleepy haze.

"Tonight you are to drive to the parking lot of the municipal library in Morton Grove. Be there promptly at 8:30. You will look for a blue Chevrolet. The license number is 784. The contact's name is Martin. He will brief you and provide everything you will need. Dress as you would for non-uniformed police work. Wear a hat. Are you with me so far?"

"I've got it."

"Read it back to me."

Wagner complied unenthusiastically.

"You're going to make an arrest. The subject is a drug dealer. He specializes in kids in their early teens."

"Is there some reason why the police can't handle this," asked Wagner.

"If they could handle it, we wouldn't be bothering. This pusher has been arrested many times, but nobody has been able to get a conviction. It's a familiar story. I'm sure you've heard it before."

"Just a few times. OK, so what do we do with him?"

"Martin will tell you. You just assist on this one. You can think of it as a kind of training mission."

"All right. I'll be there."

Wagner hung up the phone. He knew that it would be pointless to try to go back to sleep, so he got up and made a pot of coffee. He wasn't hungry enough to eat breakfast yet. For a long time he just sat at the table, sipped his coffee, and thought. It was obvious to him that he had reached another crucial point in his life. Once again he was embarking upon a course which could prove dangerous rather than following the safer, easier way. How often had he made decisions like that? He remembered that as a teenager he had been studious and liked to read, but his friends had coaxed him into trying out for the football team. Unwilling to lose face with his peers, he had gone out and practiced with the others. His football career had ended rather abruptly, however, when a big lineman ran into his knee. So much for athletic stardom.

Realizing that there wasn't much demand for 150-pound guards, he had tried track. He was never quite fast enough to be a sprinter or dedicated enough to be a distance runner, but he enjoyed running for its own sake. He had never been a particularly gregarious boy, and running alone suited his temperament. He competed with himself, trying to run farther or faster than he had run before, but seldom caring how far or how fast anyone else could run.

He had graduated near the top of his high school class and attended the state university. Leaving home was an easy transition for him. He had few close friends, and he had never established an intimate relationship with his parents. With fewer distractions than most students, he was able to focus his attention on his education. His years at the university were some of the most enjoyable of his life. He was fascinated with many areas of learning, including world literature, classical mythology, history, anthropology, and music. He was fairly good at math and the applied sciences, but was less inclined to pursue them. He surprised everyone by majoring in criminal justice as a response to his concern for several societal issues.

After his graduation from the university, he anticipated being drafted into the Army and headed off the inevitable by enlisting. His degree in criminal justice resulted in his assignment to the military police. His three years in the Army consisted of tours of duty in Germany and Fort Lewis, Washington. His MP experience led him to a position in law enforcement. Again, rather than seek a comfortable job in a smaller community, he applied for a position on the vice squad of the Chicago police force.

Wagner was diverted from his reflections by the sound of a truck outside. He stretched and grinned to himself.

"So now I'm working for an eccentric old judge who makes scrap metal out of Cadillacs just because it amuses him. What next?"

Wagner tried to stay busy that day, but time tended to drag. He wasn't especially apprehensive about the assignment, but he was anxious to get it over with. He read for a while, listened to the evening news, and ate a light supper. Eventually the time came for him to leave. He dressed as he had been instructed, knocked the dust off his seldom-worn hat, and left the apartment.

It was early evening as he drove through downtown Chicago. The rush-hour crowd was gone, and the night people had not yet appeared. This was the part of Chicago that visitors remembered, the big city with the bright lights and tall buildings. It was not the part of the city where a member of the vice squad did most of his work. That would be mostly to the south and sometimes the west. But now Wagner was out of the squalor of the vice squad routine and heading away from the most crime-ridden part of the metro area. Nonetheless, his purpose was much the same. It seemed that the more prosperous northern suburbs had their share of problems, too.

Morton Grove is just north of Chicago. Wagner drove a short distance up Interstate 94 and turned off opposite Skokie. He located the public library in Morton Grove and reached his destination before the appointed time, but he avoided entering the parking lot before 8:30. As he pulled into the lot, he found the blue Chevrolet already there. Wagner parked his car and walked over to the Chevy. The driver rolled down his window.

"You Martin?" Wagner asked.

"Yep. Leave your car there and come with me."

Wagner did as he was told. Martin left the lot and drove slowly in an easterly direction.

"I hear you're an ex-cop," said Martin.

"That's right."

"This will be easy for you. Tonight you're a cop again. Here's your badge and ID. We're making a bust."

Neither of the men talked much after that. It was apparent that each was somewhat apprehensive about the whole situation, and neither was anxious to identify himself to the other. The man called Martin didn't say any more until they were on the other side of Interstate 94 in Skokie.

"You're here to learn tonight. I'll do the talking. You just back me up."

"What are we supposed to do with this pusher?" asked Wagner.

"Nothing too rough. Personally, I'd go a lot tougher on a creep who starts little kids on hard drugs."

That was all he had to say about it. Wagner would have felt a lot more comfortable then if he had known what was going to happen after the arrest, but he resisted the impulse to ask.

At about 9:30 they pulled up in front of an apartment

house. The two men got out of the car. For the first time it occurred to Wagner that both of them, wearing long coats and dark hats, looked quite inconspicuous. Both were of medium height. Neither had any particularly prominent features. If a casual observer were to describe them it would sound something like: "Two male Caucasians, average height and build, dark hair covered by their hats, no distinguishing features such as scars or moustaches." That description would have covered about two million suspects in the greater Chicago area.

Martin led the way to an apartment on the fourth floor and knocked on the door. Eventually a short, balding man in a flannel shirt opened the door.

"Mr. Massey, I have a warrant for your arrest," said Martin as he held up his identification.

"Oh, shit! Not again!" replied the pusher.

"Get your coat. It's chilly outside."

"I want to call my lawyer first," he replied stubbornly.

"You can call him from the station."

"I know my rights. I'm entitled to a call."

"How would you like to have all your neighbors know where you're going?" asked Martin.

Massey hesitated for a moment, then said, "Forget it. I'll be back here before they're in bed. But my lawyer will teach you to screw around with me like this."

Martin didn't change expression. "Put on your coat and get moving! You're wasting our time. We'll skip the cuffs as long as you behave yourself."

Massey did as he was told, but muttered a steady stream of profanity. Wagner could hardly believe how easy it was so far. But then, Massey had obviously had a lot of practice at being arrested. The three men walked down the flight of stairs and got into the car. Wagner rode in back with Massey while Martin drove.

"Hey, what kind of a police car is this anyway?" the prisoner asked. "It doesn't even have a radio."

"Why don't you just be quiet and go along for the ride," Martin advised.

Wagner was certain that the man called Martin either was or had been a police officer.

"Damned cops can't even afford squad cars anymore." Massey was obviously nervous despite his feeble attempt at bravado. A few minutes later he exclaimed, "Hey, this isn't the way to the police station. Where are you guys taking me?"

"I told you to shut up," growled Martin. "If you don't, my partner back there will put his foot in your mouth."

Massey started to say something else about his lawyer, but thought better of it. He kept quiet until Martin pulled up in front of a school building.

"Why are we stopping here?" asked Massey, now obviously frightened.

"We thought you might like to pay one last visit to this school. After all, you made a lot of money here."

Massey panicked and started to yell, but Wagner grabbed him and stuffed a rag into his mouth. The two men half carried the struggling drug dealer to the flag pole in front of the school. Then Martin produced a pair of handcuffs and used them to secure Massey to the pole with his hands behind his back.

"Now you can call your lawyer," taunted Martin. Wagner stepped back, feeling increasingly apprehensive about not knowing what was going to happen next.

Martin unfastened Massey's belt and unzipped his trousers, then pulled his pants down. The pusher tried vainly to defend himself with his feet until his trousers were down around his ankles. Then Martin pulled out a can of spray paint from his coat pocket, shook it vigorously, and proceeded to work on the lower half of Massey's body. The victim squirmed and made animal-like noises through the gag as the cold paint coated his legs and lower body.

"Hold still or I'll paint your ugly face, too!" growled Martin. He kept painting until Massey was a bright yellow from the waist down. When he was finished, he placed the can in a plastic bag and put it back in his pocket. Then he spoke to the trembling pusher.

"I expect the police will find you and get you loose before you die of exposure. I'm sure they'll be sympathetic when they find out who you are. They'll probably volunteer to help clean you up. A gallon of turpentine should get the paint off. I recommend steel wool and lots of turpentine. That should do it. Especially around your crotch."

Martin turned away and nodded at Wagner. Then he spoke to Massey again.

"As you can see, there are some people who don't have a very high opinion of your business practices, Mr. Massey. In fact, the local Better Business Bureau is quite upset with you. Some of these people have gone to a lot of trouble to arrange this evening's entertainment. I won't even leave it to your imagination to figure out what will happen to you if you don't find a more suitable line of employment. I'll tell you what will happen. Next time we'll cut your miserable throat. You just think about it. Have a nice evening."

Massey was such a pathetic sight that it was difficult for Wagner to imagine him as a threat to anyone. But as a veteran of the vice squad, he knew better.

The trip back to the parking lot was uneventful, and neither man spoke. When they reached Wagner's car, the latter said, "Thanks for the ride."

"Don't mention it. You did just fine. Maybe we'll work together again some time."

"Who knows?" Wagner shrugged non-committally.

"We aren't always this closed-mouthed. It's just that you're new, and we try to minimize the risk."

"That figures. But what about Chief Yellow-Ass back there? If somebody doesn't find him soon, he could freeze."

"I'll call the local police right after you leave and give them an anonymous tip. We don't want some teacher finding him like that tomorrow morning."

"Right. Well, it's nearly my bedtime. Best I call it a night."

Wagner drove home with confused thoughts swirling in his head.

3

The next day Wagner's sleep was not interrupted by an early-morning phone call, and so he slept late. He got up a little before eight, turned on the radio to the FM classical music station, ate a leisurely breakfast, and puttered around the apartment until noon. He scanned the <u>Chicago Tribune</u> for any indication of his activities the previous evening, but found none. He considered calling Fletcher, his former partner on the force, to see if the latter had heard anything about it, but couldn't think of any way to ask without compromising himself.

After lunch he got into his car and maneuvered his way to Lakeshore Drive. It was a pleasant spring day, probably the nicest since the preceding October. The radio station was playing a Schubert symphony as he headed north. Wagner recognized it as the famous <u>Unfinished Symphony</u>. He hummed along in a modest baritone, marveling once again at a composer who had written roughly a thousand musical compositions in a lifetime that ended short of thirty-two years. It suddenly occurred to him that he had now lived longer than Schubert without having done anything memorable.

For perhaps the hundredth time, Wagner mulled over in his mind the gravity of the situation in which he now found himself. Actually he felt quite ambivalent about his position. On the one hand, he was in effect breaking the law by carrying out punishment without due process. On the other hand, he found it gratifying to be able to punish a criminal without having to navigate the maze of rules which the system had prescribed. Rosie was not the first felon who had escaped punishment after Wagner and his associates had built a supposedly air-tight case. Wagner thought of the radio mysteries he had listened to as a boy. When the radio detective caught the killer, there was no doubt that the latter would be convicted and sentenced. The possibility just didn't exist for someone to say, "Wait a minute! There has been a procedural error." Nick Carter and Sam Spade just didn't function that way. That was the difference between fiction and reality. Until now. Judge Carrol had changed all that. Now the absolute justice of the fiction story was attainable. Once the criminal was caught, he could be punished. Better still, the felon who had managed to elude prosecution through devious means could be punished. Scheming defense attorneys could be circumvented. Wagner found the possibilities of this new situation totally fascinating. He knew that he couldn't quit yet. He turned around and headed back toward the city. Acting upon a rather corny impulse, he turned off the radio, rolled down the window, and sang a song at the top of his lungs from Gilbert and Sullivan's Mikado:

"My object all sublime, I shall achieve in time,
To let the punishment fit the crime,
The punishment fit the crime…"

He couldn't remember any more of the words, so he just bellowed the tune until his throat hurt. Then he laughed self-consciously and turned the radio back on.

"Music should be left to musicians," he mused.

♦ ❖ ♦

The next morning the telephone rang again. Wagner glanced at the luminous dials of the clock as he picked up the receiver. It was 5:47. "Wagner here."

"Good morning, Mr. Wagner," said a voice which sounded

like neither the judge nor the last caller. "This is Benjamin. We have another job for you tonight."

"I'm listening," Wagner replied.

"We have a rapist this time. A multiple offender."

"One of my favorite people. Any arrests?"

"Only as a juvenile. He got off to an early start, it seems. Since he was only sixteen at the time, he was placed on probation. That was nine years ago. Now we know of four recent incidents, and there is strong evidence that he was involved in more than that."

"Won't any of them testify against him?"

"No. He's a high school drama teacher named Ausman. He plays up to some of his female students with flattery, gets them to stay late after rehearsal, seduces them, then threatens to ruin their reputations if they tell anyone."

"Then how can you be sure about him?"

"The girls might not be willing to testify against him, but two of them told their friends. We were able to confirm all four cases by promising to handle the matter discreetly."

"What do you want me to do?"

"This will be similar to the Massey incident, only a little rougher. Your partner will have the particulars."

"OK. Where and when?"

"You'll work with a woman this time. She'll be able to recognize Ausman. He'll be at the Hula Bar in Cicero tonight. You and your partner will persuade him to leave with you. She'll know where to take him."

"And how will I recognize my partner?"

"She'll be in a green Ford station wagon around the corner from the bar at 9:20. You can call her Tanya."

"Is she experienced in this sort of thing?"

"She has some related experience. Don't worry about her. She can take care of her end. Besides, Ausman is a small man with no recent history of violence, unless you count the young girls he's seduced."

Wagner deliberated for a minute, then said, "All right. I have some misgivings about this one, but I'll trust your judgment and go along with it."

After he had hung up, Wagner reflected on the nature of his so-called misgivings. He had no qualms about the subject. He considered a rapist about as despicable as a human could be. Even the consideration that the man could be psychologically maladjusted didn't cause him too much concern. Declaring someone psychotic didn't always put the misfit out of action. Wagner had seen too many cases where a criminal was declared mentally incompetent, institutionalized for treatment, released as "cured," and then returned to his old habits. No, that possibility didn't cause him any problem. It was the part about the female partner. It wasn't simply because she was female, but rather because his contact had hedged about her experience. A woman with solid police experience would probably be fine, but this one was described as having "related experience." What was that supposed to mean? Had she been a meter maid? Maybe an ex-Campfire Girl? How many kinds of related experience could there be for a woman? She knew all the details, and he only had the general outline. Was he expected to handle the physical part while she just gave directions? The uncertainty of it plagued him all day.

With nothing to do until evening, Wagner set out to occupy himself for the day. First he put on his sweat suit and ran four miles along Lake Michigan. After he had showered and changed, he checked his bank account to find out if a deposit had been made. He was pleasantly surprised to learn that $500 had been deposited. He withdrew a hundred and set out to restock his depleted grocery supply. He took his time and went to three different stores. By the time he had finished, it was mid-afternoon. He then spent nearly two hours preparing himself a meal consisting of roast pork with three kinds of vegetable and a salad. Ordinarily he hated to cook, but this activity had nothing to do with his preferences. It was just a device to stay busy. There was no way he could eat all of the food he had prepared, and so he carefully divided it into three parts and put most of it into the freezer compartment. Then he sat down and tried to enjoy his supper. It was better than most of his attempts at cooking. He took his time cleaning up the mess in the kitchen, but still had nearly an hour to kill. He felt a great sense of relief when it was finally time to leave for his rendezvous.

Cicero is one of the suburbs that borders Chicago on the west. As he drove there, Wagner happened to recall that it had been the home of some of the most notorious gangsters of the depression era, including Al Capone. The thought deflated his ego just a bit when he considered that he was going there to help a woman catch a perverted drama teacher. And do what? Paint him purple? He still didn't know.

He reached his destination just ahead of schedule and found the green station wagon. "Tanya" was sitting behind the wheel. If Wagner had expected her to look like a Bolshoi ballerina, he was to be disappointed. She looked more like a Russian discus thrower than a dancer.

She looked nervous when Wagner approached, but relaxed somewhat when he introduced himself as her partner.

"Good. I'm glad you're on time," she said.

"I hate to be late for a date."

"Some date!" she said. "I don't know about you, but I'll be really glad when this is over."

"It must be my deodorant."

"Look, why don't you save the corn for another time. I'm really not in the mood for it right now."

"Sorry. What are we doing?"

"Go back to your car and leave the keys in the ignition.

Somebody will take it to the parking lot at Municipal Hospital. We'll take this car from here."

Wagner complied with her instructions and noticed that someone drove off with his car while Tanya was completing the briefing. It occurred to him to hope that the driver was the one who was supposed to be taking his car to the hospital lot. Tanya completed her briefing, still visibly nervous, and the two entered the bar. Walking beside her, he noticed that she was every bit as tall as he and nearly as heavy. They found a vacant booth, sat down, and ordered two draft beers. A tinny juke box was playing a soulful lament at a volume level which Wagner could only describe as offensive.

After about a minute, Wagner asked, "Is he here yet?"

"He's standing at the bar watching the news on TV," she muttered through clenched teeth. She looked so tense that Wagner was afraid she would blow their cover.

"Relax," he whispered.

She responded by giving him a furtive look.

The waitress brought their beer, and Wagner paid her. He tried to make small talk, but Tanya replied only in monosyllables, if at all. Finally he gave up on conversation and just sipped his beer as he watched Ausman out of the corner of his eye. Eventually the predictable result of beer drinking occurred, and Ausman headed for the men's room. Wagner gave him a minute's head start, emptied his glass, and followed him. Tanya finished her beer and wandered toward the front door. The restrooms were located to the right off a narrow hall. At the end of the hall was an emergency exit. Wagner knew about all of this from Tanya's briefing, including the fact that the emergency exit sign was only intended to discourage customers from leaving without paying. It was left unlocked as a fire precaution.

Wagner had timed Ausman's bladder capacity fairly closely. The latter came out of the men's room just as Wagner approached it. Abruptly Wagner pulled out a small pistol and said, "Not a sound! Just turn around and walk out the back door."

Ausman hesitated for a second, started to raise his arms, lowered them, and did as he had been told. After a few steps, they were outside in the alley.

"I only have a few dollars," said Ausman, obviously thinking that he was about to be robbed.

Wagner ignored the remark. "To your right and no foolishness. I'm not alone."

Ausman walked to the end of the alley as he had been instructed. The station wagon was parked just across the street. Tanya was standing by it. She produced a pair of handcuffs and secured Ausman's hands behind his back. The drama teacher looked utterly bewildered, but didn't say anything. He apparently assumed that it wouldn't do any good. According to their plan, they pushed Ausman into the back seat, and Tanya got in from the other side. Wagner got behind the wheel. He didn't especially like that arrangement, but Tanya had insisted on it, and this was her show. Shortly after he drove away, he noticed a strong smell of chloroform. Apparently Tanya wasn't taking any chances.

Wagner's instructions called for him to drop south about four miles to Interstate 55 and head back to Chicago. Traffic was light, and the trip started smoothly. But they had only gone a short distance on the interstate when Tanya told him to turn off and head north.

"Where are we going?" he asked.

"Municipal Hospital."

"Already?"

"Yes. Your car is there."

"What about Ausman?"

"We'll leave him in this one. It's his car."

"Then I'll have to take you somewhere in mine."

"Yes. I'll need a ride downtown." Her voice was calm. Maybe too calm.

Wagner pulled into the hospital parking lot and drove to the far end. It occurred to him that a hospital parking lot was a good place for them to conduct their business. People were coming and going all hours of the day and night, and nobody paid much attention to anyone else. He located his car and parked two spaces away from it.

"OK, now what do we do?" he asked.

"We've already done it," was the reply.

Wagner looked back and found out what she meant. Ausman was sitting with his head tilted back, still unconscious. His trousers were pulled down below his knees. His legs were smeared with blood. Tanya had castrated him.

"Oh, my God!" Wagner heard himself say. He felt very sick to his stomach.

"Let's go," she said mechanically. "He'll wake up in a few minutes and start hollering."

Wagner climbed numbly out of the car, got into his own as Tanya entered from the passenger side, and drove away. For the first few minutes he was driving by reflex action only, but he was shaken out of his stupor by the realization that Tanya was sobbing uncontrollably. It struck him as inconsistent, but he didn't feel like asking her anything.

After a few minutes she said, "I waited nine years to get him. I thought it would be a great feeling, but it isn't. It's awful. Just awful." And she sobbed some more.

Wagner was driving in the general direction of downtown Chicago, but it occurred to him that he didn't know where he was supposed to be taking Tanya.

"Where do you want me to take you?" he asked.

She hesitated. "Can you just keep driving for a while? I need to get my head on straight."

"Would you like to get some coffee?"

"I can't go into a café looking like this."

"I'll get some at a fast food place, and you can drink it in the car."

"Thanks," she said and made a feeble attempt to smile.

Wagner found a drive-in café and bought two cups of coffee in Styrofoam containers. Tanya slurped noisily on hers.

"Would you like to tell me about it? It might make you feel better."

She was slow to respond. "I haven't talked to anyone about it for a long time," she said. She took another sip of her coffee, then began.

"First, you wondered about my experience in police work. You wanted to make sure that I could handle my end of the job. You didn't ask, but you wanted to. I could tell. Well, I don't have any. I worked for five years in a mental hospital. Because of my size, I was assigned the job of handling the most violent patients. That's why nobody hesitated to use me on this kind of an operation."

"This wasn't your first assignment for these people, was it?" Wagner asked.

"No, I went on two simpler jobs for experience. This operation was my reason for getting involved at all, though. Now that it's over, I'm moving as far away as I can get."

"Ausman meant something to you, didn't he?"

Again she hesitated. "I was probably the first woman he raped. You may think that sounds unlikely, since I'm bigger than he is. I was also bigger nine years ago, but he held a knife to my throat, and that made him ten feet tall. He came to my door one afternoon and asked to use the bathroom. He was just a kid, and I wasn't much more than that. As soon as I let him in, he pulled a knife and told me to take my clothes off. I cried and begged, but he didn't care. He raped me right there on the floor, then carved a letter A on my stomach. I'd read <u>The Scarlet Letter</u> in high school and thought he was marking me like the woman in the story, but later I found out that it was his initial. The little bastard wanted to leave his mark on me like I was his calf or something. He did, all right, but not the way he meant.

"I reported the incident to the police. When they found out how small he was, they asked me why a girl my size would submit without a struggle. They really gave me a rough time. But they caught him anyway, and he admitted doing it. I thought I'd at least have the satisfaction of seeing him punished, but it turned out that he was only sixteen years old. Since he was a juvenile with no previous record and had responsible parents, the court just put him on probation for a year. I'll never forget the dirty look his mother gave me when she left the courtroom.

"So I tried to make a life for myself. I could function all right at work, but I had no social life. I haven't been able to stand having a man touch me since that afternoon nine years ago. Then a few weeks ago I was contacted by someone from this crazy organization we're working for. You know what I mean. He told me what Ausman was doing at the school and asked me to help stop him. I just couldn't say no."

Wagner drank the last swallow of his coffee, but found that it was cold.

"Did they tell you to make a eunuch of him?" he asked.

"That was my idea, but they didn't discourage it. You don't like it, do you?"

Wagner thought for a minute. "It shocked me because I didn't know it was going to happen. In retrospect, though, I can't say that it was inappropriate. I'm glad you were able to make a positive identification, though. Can you imagine if we'd gotten the wrong man?"

"We didn't," she said grimly. "I've remembered exactly what he looked like every day for the last nine years."

"Maybe you'll be able to forget him now. I hope so. I think

you have the right idea about moving away from here. Get a new job and meet new people. Get this thing behind you. Don't let this thing ruin your whole life."

"I'm sure you're right. Oddly enough, the money I've earned from this business will make all that possible."

"Good. Are you ready to go home now?"

"Yes. Will you take me to Union Station?"

"I'll take you home if you like."

"Thanks, but that's not necessary. You've been very understanding and patient with me. I'm sorry if I was so bitchy earlier. But I'd still be more comfortable if you didn't know where I live."

"Sure. I understand. Union Station it is."

4

When the phone rang the next morning, Wagner was tempted to let it ring. Finally his curiosity won out, though, and he picked up the receiver.

"Good morning, Mr. Wagner. Benjamin," came a voice which did not sound like any of the others.

"If you say so," he replied moodily.

"You sound a bit out of sorts this morning."

"Let's just say that I'm getting tired of surprises."

"That's understandable. Next time…"

"Hold it!" Wagner interrupted. "I'm not sure there's going to be a next time. The first excursion was false arrest and simple assault. The second was more like kidnapping and practicing medicine without a license. I can hardly wait to hear what you folks have cooked up next."

"How would you like to have your job back?"

Wagner was speechless for a moment. "You're kidding," was all he could think to say.

"No, we're working on that possibility. Meanwhile, we have another project for you, if you're still interested."

"You tell me what kind of a 'project' you have in mind, and I'll tell you how interested I am. But I want it straight up front. No more surprises."

"Fair enough. What do you know about the protection racket?"

"I wasn't on the vice squad so I could run for vice president."

"All right. We're considering putting a certain undesirable

element out of action. You and a partner will run a small business in a high risk area. You're sure to be contacted by the local protection agency. We'd like to make that their last contact. In addition to ridding the world of two parasites, it would also send a powerful warning message to their associates."

"That sounds pretty final. Do you mean final like in terminal?"

"That's a distinct possibility."

"Protection goons are usually the dregs of organized crime. They can't be used for the numbers racket because they can't count past ten without taking their shoes off."

"That agrees with our assessment."

"Then why risk messing around with organized crime just to hit on some big dummies?"

"Some of these 'big dummies' have gotten quite obnoxious. They have a whole area of the city terrorized to such an extent that no one will report them or testify against them."

"Sounds like more of my kind of guys. OK, I'll probably regret it, but I'm in. When do I start?"

"You'll meet your partner tomorrow. You'll be operating a discount shoe store. Today you might want to visit some shoe stores to learn something about the way a shoe clerk handles customers."

"Any idea how long it might take before we're contacted by the thugs?"

"Probably no more than two weeks. They're quite efficient that way."

"Meanwhile I can learn a trade. My mother would be proud."

"No doubt."

"What's my partner's name?"

"Barry."

"First name or last?"

"Does it matter?"

"Not especially."

"You'll receive another call tomorrow with more specific instructions. Good luck."

"Thanks. I guess."

"Oh, one more thing."

"What's that?"

"I promised you no more surprises, so I'd better answer your last question. Barry would have to be your new partner's surname. She's a woman."

Wagner heard the receiver click before he could say anything else. His contact probably didn't care to hear any possible objection he might have to working with another female partner. Actually Wagner didn't have any objection on principle. A woman working in a shoe store might help disguise the trap.

He spent the rest of the day catching up on personal matters. Since he would be working full-time in a shoe store for the next several days, it seemed like a good idea to pay all the bills and run some errands. He took all his dirty clothes to a coin-operated laundry. He wouldn't need a suit for a while, so he took both of his to a dry cleaner and left them there. Then he visited three shoe stores and watched the sales personnel wait on various customers. He observed that there was quite a variety of professionalism in this field. Patience was a key factor, especially when the customers were women. Wagner wondered how he would react when a woman tried on a dozen pairs of shoes but didn't buy any of them. He wasn't anxious to find out.

Finally he went back to his apartment and caught up on his neglected correspondence. The letters were necessarily short because of the nature of his activities and because it wasn't his custom to write about routine matters. His relationship with his parents had become increasingly perfunctory over the years. They had never been able to relate to his interests, nor he to theirs.

The next morning he got up before seven and fried some eggs for breakfast. As usual, they were too hard, but he ate them anyway. He took his time reading the <u>Tribune</u>, wishing he knew when he could expect to be contacted. He didn't have to wonder for long, though because his phone rang at eight-thirty. A female voice gave him an address and said she would meet him at nine. The address was about five miles from Wagner's apartment house in a neighborhood that had once been mainly Italian and Polish, but which was now inhabited mostly by minority types.

Wagner drove to the address he had been given and found a parking place within three blocks. The rendezvous point was a rather shabby business site with plywood covering the windows. The door was open a crack, so he went in. The room was dusty, apparently having been used as a clothing store by the last occupants some time back. Some of the sales signs were still displayed.

The sound of his entry brought his new business partner out of the back room. She was a tall, pleasant-looking woman of about thirty-two with medium-length brown hair.

"Miss Barry?" Wagner asked.

"Mrs. Barry," she replied cheerfully. "And you must be Mr. Barry."

"How's that?" he asked, somewhat taken aback.

"I assumed that we would be setting up a sort of 'Mom and Pop' enterprise here. Wasn't that your understanding?"

"I can't say that the possibility had occurred to me, but I suppose it's as good as any."

"You really know how to flatter a lady," she said. "I don't offer to be just anyone's wife, you know."

"I should hope not," he said, for lack of anything more specific to say.

"Our inventory is due to arrive the day after tomorrow. Someone else will set up the store, but we have to get the place cleaned up by then. Our guiding light decided that it would look more realistic if we did it ourselves."

"How thoughtful of him!" observed Wagner dryly.

"The place could use a coat of paint, but they prefer that we maintain this early American décor," she said, looking around with an expression of hopelessness.

"That's fine with me," he replied. "Interior painting isn't one of my favorite indoor activities."

"I won't ask what is," she said, but instantly appeared to regret having said it. She quickly changed the subject.

"There are plenty of cleaning supplies in the back. I forgot to tell you to wear old clothes, but I see you did anyway."

"What do you mean? This is my second-best outfit."

She looked a little embarrassed for a second until he grinned.

"I'd say we're off to a rather flippant start, considering the purpose of our business venture," she remarked.

"Well, if we're going to be on that kind of terms, maybe I'd better find out what to call you. Our clientele might get suspicious if I call you Mrs. Barry."

"I suppose you're right. What would you like to call me?"

"You mean I get to name you? I feel like Pygmalion."

She frowned at that. "Well, you can't call me Galatea. Try again."

"Now how did you know about that," he asked.

She smiled coyly. "I'm full of surprises. But I still need a name."

He looked at her appraisingly and thought for a minute.

"I think you look like a Sylvia."

"Have you ever known a Sylvia?" she asked.

"No," he replied.

"Then how do you know what one looks like?"

"I have a hyperactive imagination."

"That's not good enough. Why Sylvia?"

Wagner smiled and looked a little embarrassed. "I'm partial to classical music. One of Schubert's songs is called 'Who is Sylvia?' in English. Since I don't know who you are and probably won't, it seems appropriate."

She looked pensive for a moment. "First Pygmalion, then Schubert. I have to admit, you're hardly what I expected."

"Likewise, I'm sure. But now it's your turn. What are you going to call me?"

She looked him up and down as if he were a prospective slave on an auction block. Finally she said, "I think you look like a Richard."

"Fine," he shrugged. "Will it be Dick, Rick, or what?"

"No nicknames. Richard," she said with a tone of finality.

He thought about it for a minute, then grinned impulsively.

"If you knew what my real name is, you'd get a chuckle out of your choice."

"Why? Are you Somebody the Third?"

"Nothing that Shakespearean."

"There you go again! Where did you go to school?"

"Let's just say I studied more than criminal justice. Can we live with Richard and Sylvia Barry?"

"I'd say they sound more like a couple from the social register than two people running a discount shoe store."

"True. Maybe they were disinherited."

"There you go. Down-and-out aristocrats."

"Well, while we're feeling shabby, maybe we can get this place cleaned up."

"Right," she said. "What size mop do you take?"

"I'm not sure I've ever been properly measured."

She gave him another appraising look. "You look like a 42 long. You're in luck. I just happen to have one in your size."

"Terrific! I'm allergic to dust."

And so began a strange relationship between two people who made jokes as they set a trap and established a congenial relationship without knowing each other's identity. Each morning Wagner picked up his "wife" at a bus stop, and every evening he took her back there to give any casual observer the impression that they were going home together.

Their working situation was far from easy. They cleaned up the old store as best they could by the time their shelves and merchandise arrived. It became immediately obvious that someone had bought up the inventory of a failed business. It consisted of an odd assortment of dress shoes made in Hong Kong and Italy, boots from Mexico and Spain, and sports shoes from Taiwan and Korea, none of them with recognizable brand names. There was no point in trying to measure anyone's feet for sizing, because the numbers in the shoes were totally capricious. They just let people try on shoes until they found a pair that fit. But that was hardly their biggest problem. Due to the unsavory nature of the neighborhood, the store drew a large number of kids whose only purpose was to steal sports shoes. The managers tried to counter this by displaying only the right shoe of each pair, but often these were stolen. The kids would steal the display shoe, then check the garbage cans at night to see if the mate had been thrown out. During the last two hours of each working day, one of the managers would have to stand between the merchandise and the store in order to prevent wholesale larceny. Saturdays were so bad, with all the kids out of school, that they decided to close at noon regardless of appearances.

As they were driving home after work on their second such Saturday, Wagner asked Sylvia if she would go out to dinner with him.

"Why, Mr. Barry," she replied. "I thought you were the kind of man who never takes his wife out to eat."

"Well, usually I am," he admitted, "But occasionally I make an exception."

"In that case, I'd better take advantage of your fit of generosity. I need time to run a few errands, but I could be ready by eight."

"She gets too hungry for dinner at eight…"

"That's why the lady is a tramp. I didn't know Sinatra rated in your classical repertoire."

Wagner shrugged. "Probably a carry-over from my misspent youth."

She grinned at him mischievously. "You'll have to tell me about your misspent youth. Somehow I can't picture you as ever being younger than twenty."

"That's because I wasn't born until I was sixteen years old," he managed to say with a straight face.

"I knew it! Your parents were rich and famous and couldn't be bothered with small children."

"You're guessing all my secrets," he said. "I'll have to get mysterious again or I won't have any left."

"That would spoil all my fun. I'll have to work on you this evening."

By then they had reached her bus stop.

"I'll see you at eight," he said.

"Make it seven-thirty. I get too hungry for dinner at eight."

"I'll try. See you then."

As Wagner drove back to his apartment building, he reflected on the nature of the situation. For nearly two weeks he had been working at a job which bored him beyond belief with a woman who made it almost enjoyable. She did her share of the work, maintained a congenial attitude, made pleasant conversation, and all the while was plotting with him to kill somebody. It strained his imagination to picture her doing anything violent, but he could just as well have said the same thing with respect to her perceived image of him. He had also done his share of the work, remained cheerful, engaged in witty conversation, and in general acted more like a public relations man than a hit man. Yes, she would find it equally difficult to imagine him in the latter role.

At precisely seven-thirty Wagner reached the bus stop again. Sylvia was there. He reached across the front seat to open the door for her. She got in, and they drove away.

"I was really getting hungry," she said. "Does that make me a tramp?"

"Not this lady," he replied.

"Oh, good. I like to think that I'm more sophisticated than that."

"You also look very nice."

"Thank you, kind sir."

"You'll undoubtedly be the best-dressed lady in the whole pizza parlor."

"Oh, we're going first class then."

"Nothing but. You can even have mushrooms and anchovies."

"How thoughtful of you! I'm overwhelmed!"

"Actually there's a new Armenian restaurant I've been wanting to try."

"Does that mean I don't get a pizza?"

"Some other time. I wouldn't want to spoil you all at once."

And so the conversation went as they drove across Chicago. They found the new restaurant, parked in the lot, and went inside. The restaurant was small, but tastefully decorated. A waiter escorted them to a table and took their order for drinks. Sylvia smiled as she stirred her drink.

"I wonder what our business associates would think about our socializing."

"Why should they care? They didn't object to our being married, did they?"

She wasn't in the mood for their usual game of wits just then. "Have you ever been married before?" she asked.

"No. Engaged twice. Never married. You?"

"I was married for five years."

An awkward silence followed because Wagner was reluctant to ask the obvious question, and Sylvia didn't elaborate. Finally he broke the tension by asking, "Do you suppose we can get an Armenian pizza?"

She wrinkled her nose at that suggestion. "I'd like something with an exotic name I can't pronounce. And I don't want to know what it is. Especially if it's goat."

"That sounds like half the items on the menu."

She laughed and touched his hand. Now she was ready for more verbal fencing, and he suddenly felt serious.

"Do you realize what we're doing?" he asked. "Since we have to remain virtual strangers to each other, we compensate with a lot of inane chatter."

"Yes," she replied, "But neither of us can keep it up for long without getting analytical about it. I've noticed that several times."

"Has it ever occurred to you that we make a very unlikely pair to be in this situation?"

She looked at him soberly. "Richard, any two people would be an unlikely pair for this situation."

He shook his head. "At least I know why I'm doing it. I can't imagine why you are."

"I could have said exactly the same line."

The statement didn't surprise him, but he found it gratifying nonetheless.

"Just where do you think I belong, Richard?" she asked.

He thought for a moment. "If I had met you under different circumstances, I would have taken you for a professor of English literature at an exclusive private college. Or maybe classics."

She smiled, pleased at his response. "And you could pass for a professional man—or maybe a rising executive."

"Hardly. I just have an undergraduate degree in criminal justice."

"And I dropped out of grad school to get married. Not English lit or classics either. Political science and sociology."

"What were you planning to do with that?"

"Nothing in particular. It just interested me. I wasn't all that concerned about the working world. My father was a doctor, and he sent me to Radcliff. I grew up with just about everything I wanted."

"OK. I give up. I can't imagine why you're in this."

"Why don't you tell me what you're doing here and I'll do the same."

Wagner sipped his drink and tried to think where to begin. "As I said, I majored in criminal justice at the university. Just how I came to do that would be hard to explain. I guess it started with some vague notion of becoming a parole officer. I had some idea of making a contribution to society and thought I might be suited for counseling people in trouble with the law. As soon as I graduated, I could see the draft coming and enlisted in the Army. They assigned me to the Military Police. After a tour in Germany, they gave me some schooling in drug control and sent me to Sixth Army—that's the west coast—as a narcotics specialist. That led to a job on the Chicago police force after I was discharged. Being a sucker for taking risks, I volunteered for the newly formed vice squad task force.

"I don't know why I keep doing these things. I'm barely tall enough to meet the minimum five-ten requirement. I'm a lousy shot with a pistol no matter how much I practice. Maybe that's why they gave me a partner who looks like a one-man wrecking crew and is deadly with just about any weapon.

"I'm not used to talking about any of this. I've thought about it to the point of obsession, but it's hard to put it into words."

She nodded understandingly, and he continued. "You know how it is in fiction. Crime doesn't pay—the Shadow knows. All that sort of foolishness. At the end of the whodunnit, the bad guy is caught, and you just know he'll get what's coming to him. Crime and Punishment. The same pattern over and over again. Well, just for the record, crime not only pays, it pays damned well. Of all the crimes committed, only a small percentage of the cases are solved, and even then most of the serious criminals are never convicted. Our legal system is more concerned with the rights of the accused than the rights of the rest of us not to have a bunch of creeps running around loose. I saw that over and over again. I finally blew my cool when a judge turned one of my prizes loose. The creep had the gall to stand there and grin at me as if he were thumbing his nose at our whole impotent system. I hit him. That cost me my job and drew the attention of our mutual acquaintance."

She looked at him for a moment, then said, "What a couple of paradoxes we are! We both enjoy good food and fine culture, yet we've both gotten ourselves caught up in the muck of our society."

"Well, it's your turn. How did you get dragged into this?"

She stared at her plate for a minute while she collected her thoughts.

"It wasn't anything all that close to home," she said. "I grew up in a sheltered environment. I don't recall seeing anyone poor until I was at least twenty. The events of the sixties troubled me, but I couldn't identify with any of the problems. The trial of the Manson family bothered me quite a lot, first because of the awful crimes they committed, but also because it took nine months and enormous expense to convict those people. Then every so often I would hear about someone like Charles Manson or Richard Speck being considered for parole. That caused me to question our system in the way you mentioned. But all of that was detached and remote because it wasn't affecting me directly. Then one night I saw a woman stabbed to death. A man tried to steal her purse, but she held on to it and screamed. Even though there were people standing around, he killed her and ran away with her purse. None of us did anything to try to stop him. No one could identify him very well. As far as I know, no one even tried very hard to catch the man. I felt shocked at our system, but even more I felt impotent for not being able to do anything. Maybe I couldn't have prevented the woman's death, but I didn't even try to do anything. I just stood there in a state of shock. After that, I made several speeches at civic organizations urging reform. I don't think many people noticed, but at least one man did."

"Our mutual friend."

"Probably, but I'm not sure of anything about the structure of the organization."

"I'm not either, but we shouldn't be talking about it here. Let's see if we can find something more cheerful to discuss."

They spent the rest of the evening making small talk and exchanging witticisms. Then Wagner offered to take her closer to her home, but she insisted that he drop her off at the bus stop as usual.

"I'll be all right," she said. "Thank you for a lovely evening."

"Sure. See you Monday morning."

Wagner drove home listening to a Beethoven concerto and trying to figure out why a woman like Sylvia would get herself involved in such a risky business. He didn't come up with any answers.

5

The next Monday was a gray, rainy day with temperatures in the low forties. Traffic was moving slower than usual due to a stalled vehicle, and the "Barrys" were late getting to the store. It hardly mattered, though. They seldom had any business before eleven. They spent the early part of the day straightening up the displays that had been scattered by the previous Saturday's clientele. This time Wagner rearranged the displays while Sylvia worked with the books.

"I hope our prize customers show up pretty soon," she remarked. "Otherwise we're going to need more shoes to sell."

"We must have sold more than I thought then," he replied.

"Not really. We've sold forty-three pairs of shoes, but we're stuck with at least eighteen left tennis shoes from where the kids have stolen the right."

"Maybe when we go out of business we can run a sale for one-legged joggers."

"Or people with two left feet," she said. "I've danced with a few of those."

"Careful! You're hitting close to home."

"Oh, I'll bet you're a good dancer."

"No, I'm not. Some time I'll take you out and prove it to you."

"In that case, maybe I should keep a pair of those steel-toed boots."

"My high school sweetheart used to wear those."

Their conversation was interrupted by a big man in a shabby blue suit who entered the store.

"Yes, sir, may I help you?" asked Wagner in his best business manner.

"Actually, I'm here to help you," said the big man.

"Really? How's that?"

"I'm in the property insurance business. I see that you're new to the neighborhood. You'll probably find that it isn't easy to get property insurance here. It's considered a high-risk area."

"So we're told. What company do you represent?"

"It's an independent company. We're small, but we cover most of the businesses in this area."

"What kind of coverage do you offer?"

"Fire, theft, vandalism, the usual."

"And how much does a policy cost?"

"For a place this size, I'd say a hundred a month."

Wagner let out a low whistle. "That sounds pretty high."

"Like I said, this is a high-risk area."

"We'll have to think about it. Why don't you leave us a copy of your policy and your business card, and we'll call you if we decide to do business with you."

The man frowned. "I don't have a copy with me right now. I'll be back tomorrow."

"All right. We'll look over your policy, but we'll want to compare prices with other companies before we decide."

The man gave Wagner a strange look, but said, "Yeah, you do that."

As soon as he had left, Wagner went to the door. "No car in sight. He's probably making the rounds. There's another man with him now. Must be a look-out."

"He's our man," she stated grimly. "His name is Scales. His friend there is Hulsman."

She went to the phone, dialed a number, and waited for an answer. "This is Mrs. Barry. We need a delivery tomorrow. Fine." That was all.

There was no more joking that day. There wasn't much conversation at all. Both of them knew what had to be done. The waiting was over. They had rehearsed the details of their main plan and several contingencies. There wasn't anything more to say about the matter. But it was a grim business, and they were both tense.

The next morning found them in much the same state. Neither had slept well. Neither spoke much, both of them lost in their own private thoughts. It was another day, and it dragged on at a snail's pace. Morning stretched into noon, but neither made a move to take a lunch break. What if he didn't come back that day? Another curious dichotomy. While they instinctively dreaded seeing the man again, the alternative was another tense, sleepless night. He said he'd come back the next day, but how much faith could they put in the word of a man like that?

Early afternoon brought a few customers. At least they helped relieve the tension. Sylvia sold two pairs of Korean shoes. Wagner went through the plan mentally for about the hundredth time. Three o'clock came. No sign of Scales. Four o'clock. Nothing. He wouldn't come that day. Nearly five. Almost time to go home. Then the door opened and a boy of about twelve came in. He wandered around the store for a minute, then started rummaging through a pile of marked-down tennis shoes. Ordinarily one of them would have taken a position between the boy and the door, but just then neither of them was especially concerned about the loss of any more inventory.

Suddenly the boy grabbed an armload of shoes and bolted for the door. He was too far away for either of them to stop him. But just as he reached the door, it opened and a man blocked the exit. At the same moment, the plate glass window of the store shattered. Someone had thrown a brick through it. The man in the doorway seized the boy by the arm, led him back to where he had stolen the shoes, made him drop them, then let him go. It was Scales.

"I told you this was a bad neighborhood," he said calmly. "You folks need protection."

"I guess we do," said Sylvia. "How much did you pay the kid to pull that stunt?"

Scales chuckled mirthlessly. "Lady, you're on the wrong track. It doesn't seem like you've been talking to the other folks who run businesses in this area."

While they were talking, Wagner pushed a button under the counter which locked the front door. It had seemed like a sophisticated device when they installed it, but it seemed less so with the front window demolished. However, it had only been intended to keep prospective customers out, so it was probably sufficient.

"We'll look at your policy now," said Wagner. "I presume that you have a copy of it this time."

Scales glared at him. "Look, dumb ass, I'll spell it out for you nice and clear. Either you pay me a hundred bucks up front and the same every month or you're out of business. You got it?"

Wagner feigned surprise. "OK, I'll get it for you," he said and walked toward the back room.

Scales was obviously taken by surprise by this maneuver. He hadn't counted on having the two of them separated.

"You go back there with him," he barked at Sylvia as he motioned her toward the back.

Sylvia walked to the back of the store with Scales right behind her. Before he could adjust his eyes to the darker back room, Wagner hit him over the head with a two-foot length of pipe. The big man dropped to the floor with his skull crushed. Deftly, Sylvia whipped out a garbage bag and pulled it over his head to keep the blood from soaking the floor.

"Now we wait for Hulsman," she said. She went back out

front and pushed the button to unlock the front door. Then she started sweeping up the broken glass from the shattered window.

A few minutes later the door opened and a smaller man with a moustache came in. He looked around, then asked, "Where's Scales?"

Sylvia replied, "Oh, the insurance salesman? He asked to use the rest room."

Hulsman mulled that over for a moment, then frowned and asked, "Where's your husband?"

"I think he's helping Mr. Scales," she answered.

Hulsman's eyes grew larger, and he rushed to the back. He was suspicious and therefore better prepared for danger than Scales, and he was also more agile. He caught a glimpse of Wagner as the latter swung the pipe, and he ducked. The pipe smashed harmlessly into a shelf. Hulsman's fist slammed into Wagner's stomach, doubling him over. But before the man could press his advantage, Sylvia grabbed him from behind with a chokehold. He struggled to free himself from her tenacious grasp as Wagner gasped for air. It was at best an uneven contest, and eventually Hulsman broke her grip. As she pressed the attack, he pulled a switch-blade knife from his pocket and slashed at her. By then she had bought enough time for Wagner to recover from the blow to his stomach, and he crashed into Hulsman from one side. Hulsman fell to the floor, half buried by an avalanche of shoes. As he struggled to stand up, Wagner kicked him in the chest. The knife dropped from his grasp, and he looked up to see the grimmest expression he had ever seen in his life. Wagner's next blow came from the heel of his right hand against Hulsman's nose. Then he grabbed the fallen man's collar with both hands and pressed his thumbs against Hulsman's throat. Hulsman convulsed and flailed wildly with his arms, but he was powerless against his grim adversary. Within fifteen seconds he stopped moving.

Wagner dropped the lifeless form and turned around to survey the damage. The back room was a shambles, but the front was practically untouched except for the window. Sylvia was on the floor trying to stand up. Only then did Wagner realize that she had been cut.

"Here, let me help you," he said.

She tried to smile. "He got me with that switch-blade."

Blood was running down her blouse, but the cut did not appear to be critical. He helped her into the small bathroom to see what could be done.

"You'd better lock the front door and turn off the lights," she said.

Wagner complied, marveling at her presence of mind under the circumstances. When he returned to her, she had removed her blood-soaked blouse and was looking in the mirror. The knife had cut her from her left shoulder blade diagonally across her right breast.

"I'd better get you to a hospital," he said.

"What would I tell them? I was shaving my under-arms when suddenly…"

The tension was broken. She was cut and he was bruised, but the suspense was gone. The job was finished.

"You could say you were an Amazon and had tried to cut off your right boob to improve your archery."

"I suppose I could. But I think I can take care of this with a little first aid and some bed rest. It isn't too deep."

"My Boy Scout training never prepared me for anything like this."

"Surely you've seen female breasts before," she teased.

"Yes, I used to look at the pictures in National Geographic when I was a boy, but my mother warned me I could go blind."

"Wonderful," she said. "Now stop carrying on and help me get my bra off before I pass out."

He unhooked her bra and added it to the growing pile of bloody clothing. He made a mental note to take it with them when they left. Then he wetted two paper towels and cleaned her wound so he could see how serious it was. It would stop bleeding without medical attention, but he quipped, "My gosh! Where do I apply the tourniquet?"

"That is a problem, isn't it? I once heard of a woman being bitten on the bottom by a poisonous snake."

"You see? There's always someone who's worse off than you."

Just then someone knocked at the back door.

"That must be our friendly delivery service," she said weakly. "If they have to use the bathroom, please direct them to the nearest filling station."

Wagner opened the back door cautiously. Two men were there with a van. "The merchandise is right here," he said.

The two men picked up the bodies and put them in the van. Then one said, "We'll be back to clean the place out after we get back from the crematorium."

Once more Wagner was struck by the extent to which the organization had exceeded his expectations. He had pictured a boat on Lake Michigan dumping two weighted bodies. But a crematorium? That had all kinds of implications. Above all, it meant that it was possible to make someone disappear with no chance of later discovery. What had ever happened to Jimmy Hoffa? Police had dug up half the country with no results. Most theories had him in a swamp, at the bottom of a lake, or buried in some remote site. Had it occurred to anyone that he might have been cremated? Maybe no one had attributed that capability to any of the most likely suspects. Wagner wasn't sure about that. But the judge's organization apparently had access to such a facility. How much did they intend to use it? Wagner decided to return to these questions when he had more time for reflection and less to do.

As soon as the bleeding stopped, Wagner gave Sylvia his shirt and went to get the car. He drove to the back door by the alley, helped her into the car, and departed the shoe business forever.

As they drove away, it was apparent that she was still in considerable pain, but she didn't complain. Wagner kept glancing her way as he drove. He needed to make a difficult decision, and there wasn't much time. By the time they reached her bus stop, he had decided. He drove right past the spot where he had left her so many times before.

"What are you doing? That was my stop," she protested. "Where are you taking me?"

"I'm not leaving you like this," he said firmly.

"But you can't take me to your place. You'll compromise your identity."

He looked at her for a moment. "Lady, whoever you are, if you think I can just drop you off at a bus stop in your condition and ride off into the sunset, you don't know me very well."

She managed a feeble smile. "I may not know who you are either, but I think I know you pretty well. Thanks, partner."

6

Wagner found a parking place in the lot behind his apartment building. As he helped Sylvia out of the car, it was evident that she was in considerable pain, but she managed a weak smile. He took her arm, and she tried to walk as erectly as possible. Their raincoats concealed the fact that she was wearing his shirt and he had on only a T-shirt for an upper garment. Both were shivering when they reached the building. They met several occupants of the building in the hall, but tried to look as nonchalant as they could under the circumstances. By the time they reached his apartment, however, she was no longer able to stand up straight. He unlocked the door, turned on the light, and maneuvered her straight toward the bedroom. As he helped her remove her raincoat, she remarked, "Do you always rush women into your bedroom so fast?"

"No, I usually offer them a drink first."

She unbuttoned his shirt carefully. The cut had started to bleed again, and part of the shirt was stuck to it.

"I'm afraid I've ruined your shirt," she said.

"I'll let you buy me a new one," he replied as he helped her peel the bloody shirt away from the wound. "We'd better clean that cut. You lie down while I get a pan of soapy water."

"Yes, Doctor."

He returned with some towels and a pan of warm water. He placed towels on either side of her and started to wash the dried blood away from the cut.

"They should give you a medal for service above and beyond the call of duty," she said.

"Oh, I do this for all the girls," he replied.

"I can't wait to see how you plan to bandage it."

"I don't have a band-aid that big. Actually I think it would be best just to apply a disinfectant and leave it uncovered until the blood clots more. A bandage would just stick to it."

"You just want to look at my chest," she teased.

"Well, that too, but right now we'd better concentrate on getting you healed up. I'll turn the thermostat up. If you're still too cold, I'll give you a light blanket."

She tried to smile. "Do you have a bullet for me to bite when you apply the disinfectant?"

"I'm fresh out of bullets. Will a clothes pin do?"

"I'm just kidding. Let's get it over with."

She gritted her teeth as he applied the caustic liquid, but didn't make a sound.

"There," he said. "That's got it. Now you have a pretty red stripe across your chest."

"Terrific! I wonder how much of a scar this will leave."

"Well, I don't think you'll want to wear a low-cut gown for a while. You'd be the only girl at the party with a diagonal cleavage."

She grinned again. "It could be worse, though. If I'd been standing a little closer to Hulsman, I'd have gotten a radical mastectomy."

It was his turn to smile. "You know, you're quite a woman."

"Does this mean that I've finally been promoted to woman? You've been calling me a girl."

He was somewhat taken aback by the remark and apologized. "Sorry. No offense intended."

"None taken. You've been very gentle and considerate of me. I realize that this must be extremely awkward for you."

"You'd think so, but oddly enough it isn't. I'll admit to all the impulses of a healthy, red-blooded American male, but this isn't that kind of a situation. My emotional range right now is limited to big-brother types of concern. No passion. No embarrassment. Just a kind of warm feeling of responsibility."

She smiled slightly. "I appreciate that, Richard. I really do. Ordinarily I'd be mortified to find myself in a position like this, but you've handled the situation quite gracefully."

Wagner blushed a little at that remark and started to pick up the extra towels and medicine. "Do you need to call anyone and let them know that you'll be delayed getting home?"

"No, I live alone. No one will miss me for a while."

"How about something to eat?"

"I'm not hungry right now. Maybe some soup later. You go ahead, though."

Wagner heated up some leftovers on the stove. By the time he had finished, she was asleep. He stood in the doorway for a minute and watched her. It occurred to him that he was supposed to be parting company with her without any way of locating her again. He suddenly found that prospect very repugnant. He had maintained a certain emotional distance because of the terms of the arrangement, but now that was changed. He tried to analyze his feelings. He hadn't fallen in love with her. She had never aroused passion in him. Even looking at her half naked, he didn't feel any sense of lust for her. What was it then? Eventually it occurred to him that she had become his best friend. It was just that simple—and that complex. She was a thoroughly likeable human being, and he enjoyed being with her. Added to that was the vulnerability of her present situation. Her customary independence was temporarily suspended by her injury, and he was responsible for her welfare. He found that he rather liked that role.

Sylvia was unable to sleep for long that night. Every time she moved in her sleep, the cut would hurt. Thus, she woke up repeatedly. Around midnight Wagner heated some soup for her, and she ate a little. Once he had to help her walk to the bathroom. It was after three before Wagner got any sleep.

It seemed as if he had just gotten to sleep when he was rudely awakened by the sound of the telephone ringing. He glanced at the clock and saw that it was 6:45. It took him a few seconds to remember why he was sleeping on the couch and why he had moved the phone to the living room.

"Hello," he muttered groggily.

"Good morning, Mr. Wagner; Benjamin here," responded a voice which sounded like none of the others he had heard before. "Sorry to disturb you so early, but I wanted to be able to reach you before you went out."

"What made you think I'd be going out before seven o'clock? I'm retired from the shoe business."

"Yes, I heard that you took care of those customers."

"You probably didn't hear that my partner got hurt in the process."

"No, I hadn't heard that. Seriously?"

"She got a bad cut. I didn't think it would be a good idea to take her to a hospital. The cut doesn't look like anything she'd be likely to get around the kitchen. So I brought her to my place."

There was a pause before the other responded.

"Then I suppose she knows who you are."

"I doubt it, but I don't really know whether she does or not. It doesn't seem especially important right at the moment. Frankly, I rather like the lady, and I'm concerned about what happens to her."

There was a sigh on the other end of the line. "You realize, of course, that your actions have probably reduced the value of both of you to the organization."

"I suppose they have."

"Well, under the circumstances, I don't imagine that you had much choice."

"Oh, I had a choice. I could have dumped her at the bus stop."

"I get your point. We'll have to do some adjusting. Meanwhile, I have news for you. You are to be reinstated on the police force. You'll receive a letter to that effect this week."

"How did you arrange that—or shouldn't I ask?"

"You shouldn't ask. I'd like for you to stay in contact as a sort of consultant. Are you still interested in our operation?"

"I guess I am. I keep having second thoughts about it, but there's something about it that appeals to me."

"Fine. You'll have a few days to rest. I think you deserve that after your latest assignment."

"Yeah. Selling shoes can be hard work."

"I can imagine. When will your partner be back in her apartment?"

"I suppose within a couple of days. She doesn't have anything here except the clothes on her back." Wagner had to wince as he said that.

"Please tell her that I'll call her in a few days. And that I wish her a speedy recovery."

"I'll do that."

"I'm quite pleased with the work you two did."

"Thanks. I'll tell my partner that." At the moment he could think of no other designation for Sylvia. He still didn't know her real name, and "Sylvia" was their private designation. Only later did it occur to him that "Benjamin" had referred to her as "Barry."

As he hung up, Sylvia called him from the bedroom. He walked over to the room and looked in on her. She had pulled the covers up to her neck.

"That was our contact, wasn't it?" she asked.

He replied in the affirmative and related the details of the conversation. Then he added, "He said you deserved a medal, but I told him I didn't know where we'd pin it."

She smiled. "I heard you say something to the effect that you didn't feel like breaking up the act. Did you mean that?"

Wagner sat down on the edge of the bed and brushed her hair away from her forehead. "Sure I meant it. Good partners are hard to come by."

She looked at him with an expression that he couldn't interpret. He leaned over and kissed her lightly on the cheek.

"Why don't you try to get some more sleep?" he said. "Tonight we'll see about getting you back to your place."

As he left her there, he knew that he wouldn't be able to sleep right away. Too much was happening too quickly. He picked up his sweat suit. He would run along the lake front until he was exhausted. Then he would be able to sleep.

7

It was early afternoon when Wagner awoke again. "Terrific!" he thought. "I'll be screwed up on my sleep for the rest of the week."

He got up from the couch and opened the curtains. The sunlight blinded him for a minute. The clouds had dispersed, even if the temperature hadn't risen by much. He went into the bathroom, relieved himself, washed his face, and shaved. Only then did it occur to him that he was quite hungry. He decided to check on his guest before preparing lunch. He walked quietly to the bedroom. Sylvia appeared to be sleeping, but the slight sound he made caused her to open her eyes.

"How are you doing?" he asked.

"Fine as long as I lie still."

"Are you hungry?"

"Not very, but I'm thirsty, though."

"What would you like?"

"What have you got?"

"All I have cold is beer and orange juice. I can make coffee or tea, though."

"A glass of orange juice sounds good."

"Anything to eat?"

"Not just yet, thanks."

He poured a glass of orange juice and brought it to her. She struggled to sit up and drink it, trying to keep herself covered up. The effort was not very effective.

"Guess I'll have to forget about maidenly modesty for now," she said.

"If it bothers you, I'll leave," he replied.

She shook her head. "I think it's too late to worry about modesty. It's nice to have you here. This would be a bad time to be alone."

The cut had already begun to heal. It did not seem that ordinary movement would cause it to bleed again. The cut formed an angry red gash across her body, but it apparently posed no immediate threat to her life.

"You can stay here as long as you like," he said. "I don't have any reason to leave for long."

She smiled. "I appreciate your hospitality as well as your medical attention, but I should get back to my place tonight. I don't even have a change of underwear here."

"I'll help you as soon as you're ready. Do you have any concern about my finding out where you live?"

"Not anymore. If you want to know anything about me, I'll tell you. But I won't volunteer much. That's because I still don't even know your real name, and I'm not particularly anxious to come all the way back to reality. We were so compatible as Richard and Sylvia Barry. I rather hate to see all that come to an end."

He took her glass and set it on the night table. "I'll be Richard Barry for as long as you like. I'd have a hard time thinking of you as anything other than Sylvia. And I don't need to know a whole lot about you. We've been through quite an adventure together, and frankly I'm really impressed by what I've seen."

She grinned impishly. "Are you talking about my personality or my body?"

He laughed. "I knew that was coming as soon as I gave you the lead."

"Well, I wouldn't want to disappoint you, would I?"

"I'll settle for your personality for now. I'll wait until you're healthy to go after your body."

"Fair enough. But why don't you go ahead and fix yourself something to eat? You must be hungry."

"You should eat something, too. Maybe you'll be hungrier by the time I get it ready."

"Could be. Why don't you help me to the bathroom. I'm still a little light-headed. Then I'll try sitting in the kitchen while you fix lunch."

Wagner complied with her request, but he went to check the mail while she was occupied. He found the letter from the department which his contact had mentioned. He read it quickly and found that he had been reinstated to the force. His absence had become in effect an unpaid suspension. Sylvia was ready to be helped to the kitchen by the time he had finished reading it. He gave her a light summer shirt to wear.

As he worked in the kitchen, he told her that he had been reinstated. She seemed surprised by the news.

"What will that do to your status with our group?" she asked.

"I'm not sure. The contact asked me to stay on as some kind of a consultant. I don't know what that's supposed to mean."

"It probably means that they want another member of their group inside the establishment," she reasoned.

"That would figure. I just hope that it doesn't lead to a conflict of interest."

"It very well could. We'll just have to reckon with that when the time comes."

"At least they've given us an easy out. We can quit at any time."

She thought about that for a moment, then said, "Have you ever considered that with each successive assignment we are getting more deeply involved in this and correspondingly less likely to get out?"

"I don't know about that. It seems to me that we can walk

away at any time." He thought of Tanya as he commented. "What do you plan to do now?"

"I was primarily involved with gathering information before this assignment. I suppose I could go back to doing that again."

"I'd like to keep your telephone number and stay in touch with you. Would that be all right?" he asked.

"Very much so. I was pleased when you were so straightforward with our contact about your rationale for keeping me with you."

"I'm not really complex enough to be devious," he said. "But I won't try to find out your name, either. I'd be devastated to learn that my Sylvia is really a Mabel."

She grinned. "And my Richard is probably a Maxwell."

"It might be worse than that."

"I wouldn't worry about it."

Wagner turned to his cooking, which was not faring well under the circumstances.

"I try not to worry about anything unless I can do something about it," he said.

"In that case, you might worry a little about those hamburgers. I think they were done quite a while ago."

Wagner salvaged their lunch, dished it up, and put it on the table. Sylvia accepted a small portion of the burnt offering. As she nibbled on the charred meat, she remarked, "There is one thing I'd like to know about you."

"What's that?"

"You said that you had been engaged twice. Why didn't you ever get married?"

Wagner shrugged. "I was too young."

"You don't have to tell me if you don't want to. I was just indulging my latent feminine curiosity."

He thought for a minute, then said, "The first time was when I was at the university. I knew I'd have to spend some time in the military and wanted to get that over with before getting married. The young lady in question didn't want to wait. Basically, I couldn't afford to support a wife, and she wasn't interested in the economics of the situation."

He went to the refrigerator, got out a bottle of beer, opened it, and poured it into a glass.

"The second time was more complicated. I really had a bad case for a woman in Denver. I was taking some special training there a few years ago. She seemed to care for me, but she didn't like my line of work. By the time we got it all sorted out, it didn't seem like such a good idea to get married."

Sylvia looked at him thoughtfully for a while, then said, "You really cut it down to the bare bones, don't you?"

The comment surprised him. "What do you mean?"

"I used to think you played it close to the vest because of the confidential nature of your work. Now I don't think so. I think that you don't want anyone to know very much about you, and it has very little to do with your work."

Wagner felt somewhat defensive. "Maybe I just find it difficult to imagine that anyone particularly cares to hear my life history. It isn't really all that thrilling."

"I didn't expect it to be thrilling. I just asked because I wanted to know more about a man who has shown me an unusual amount of tenderness and concern."

"I'm sorry if I've disappointed you. I'm just not in the habit of talking about such things."

"When you're ready, Richard. I won't press you."

Wagner finished his meal and leaned back with the glass of beer in his hand.

"While we're on the subject, would you care to tell me about your marriage?"

She took a deep breath. "I suppose I asked for that. It isn't a very pretty story, but it did comprise a significant part of my life. I was attending graduate school at Georgetown University.

My major field was political science, and Washington seemed to be the best place to study it. I met a congressional aide and fell in love with him. We got married, and I dropped out of school in order to be able to travel with him. It was an exciting life—for a while. Then the senator for whom he was working lost his bid for re-election, and my husband lost his job. He used some of my savings to try to set himself up in business, but he didn't have much business sense. He wanted more money and asked me to tap my mother's resources. It soon became evident that he expected me to finance an endless series of get-rich-quick schemes. He tried to be some kind of a wheeler-dealer, but he wasn't smart enough. Whenever I'd suggest that he look for a real job, he'd get mad. I finally got tired of financing his ventures, so I invested in a divorce lawyer instead." She hesitated for a moment. "My mother hasn't spoken to me since then."

By the time she had finished her narrative, Sylvia looked thoroughly depressed.

"I'm sorry I asked," said Wagner, "But I'm glad you told me anyway."

"I feel like such a fraud after criticizing you."

"Don't. We are what we are. And personally, I think you're pretty special. Your ex-husband sounds like some kind of a donkey. Do you think you'd be better off if you'd stayed with him?"

"No. I had to consider that before I left him."

"Then you're better off putting it behind you."

"That's easier said than done," she said. "I'll guarantee you, it's a lot rougher ending a marriage than breaking off an engagement."

"I'm sure it is. I just hate to see it depress you so much when you talk about it. You don't have to mention it again on my account."

"No, but somehow I felt that I needed to tell you about it."

"I guess I don't exactly understand that," he said.

"I'm sure you don't. You could probably go on indefinitely without telling me anything significant about where you've been or what you've done."

"I told you, I haven't done anything earth-shaking."

"There you go again! Let me tell you something. When our contact approached me about taking on this past operation, I was really apprehensive about doing it. He told me that my partner was a man who was fairly new to the system, but who was as capable as anyone he could find. Now, you don't establish that kind of a reputation by doing nothing significant."

"I didn't say I hadn't done anything. I just said that I didn't think it would be of much interest to anyone."

"Well, now you know differently."

"If you say so."

"I say so."

"I think the patient has just become the doctor."

"I think the patient is going to have to lie down before she falls down."

"Do you want the bed or the couch?"

"I'll try the couch. I'd rather talk to you than just lie there."

"Why don't you take a couple of aspirins? I don't have anything stronger for pain, but they should help some."

As he went to get the aspirins, she noticed his collection of books and records. Both were numerous and varied. When he returned, she commented on his library.

"I see you have your own Book-of-the-Month Club," she said.

"I don't really read them. I just keep them to impress my lady visitors."

"I see. And you bought three hundred classical records just for show."

"Yup. My blue-grass and rock-and-roll are in the closet."

"I'd like for you to play me something that you really like. I don't care what style."

Without hesitating, he picked out Tchaikowsky's <u>Fourth Symphony</u> and put it on the turn-table.

"That's what I thought," she said. "You play Tchaikowsky and read great literature, then feel almost apologetic about it. Why?"

He shrugged. "In some circles, that would be considered hopelessly out of date."

"In others, you'd be considered a Renaissance man."

"I don't travel in those circles."

"What kind of circles do you travel in?"

"Mostly my own, I guess. I work in a sordid world with a lot of undesirable people. When I get home, I like to tune all of that out. So I play music and read books that reflect the best of what mankind has produced. This helps me to be able to face the worst."

"Why did you go into police work in the first place? It doesn't seem very consistent with your temperament."

"I think it's consistent with one side of my nature. Somebody has to do it, and I think I'm fairly good at it. I went into law enforcement with a considerable amount of idealism and enthusiasm. A lot of that has tarnished over the years, but I still have a strong sense of purpose for what I'm doing."

"Don't you find it frustrating?"

"Sure. You start out with the idea of cleaning up a part of the world. You soon find out that you can't clean up very much of it. And while you're out there working on it, the other side is winning the war. The percentage of crime keeps increasing."

"Then why do you stay with it?"

"What if we all quit? Life wouldn't be worth living."

"I can't argue with that."

"I guess you can't. It seems to me that you're pretty heavily involved in this yourself."

"So it seems."

"And even with that cut, you haven't said anything about becoming a librarian."

"That's right."

"So we're both still in it."

"We're both still in it."

He walked over to her and gave her a kiss on the forehead. "And this latest battle has made us bosom buddies, hasn't it?"

She cringed. "I'll never hear the last of this, will I?"

8

Wagner waited until nearly nine that evening to try to move Sylvia back to her apartment. He lived near the University of Chicago and the Museum of Science and Industry. She lived about three miles north and a little west of there, closer to downtown Chicago. It was not a great distance to cover, but there was no way to avoid movement which would aggravate her wound. She was still determined to return to her own apartment, however, so he tried to make the move as painless as possible.

Sylvia stood up and practiced walking erectly in his apartment. She was a little light-headed at first, but gradually she felt better. Then they put on their coats and left the building. He helped her into his car in the parking lot. Only then did he realize how pale her face looked.

"Are you sure you're going to make it?" he asked.

"I'll be all right," she answered.

As he drove northward, it became obvious to him that she was experiencing considerable discomfort, but she didn't say anything, so he tried not to notice. She directed him to her apartment building, and he found a parking place near the back door. She appeared to be gritting her teeth as they walked to the building. They went inside, took the elevator to the fourth floor, and walked down the hall to her apartment. She handed him her key without saying anything. He unlocked the door, and they went inside. She turned on a light, then sat down in a chair without even taking off her coat.

"There's some Tylenol in the bathroom medicine cabinet," she said. "Would you please get it for me?"

Wagner found it and brought it to her with a glass of water. She took two capsules and chased them with the water. Then she started to remove her coat. The cut had begun to bleed again.

"I'll soak your shirt in cold water before it's ruined," she said.

"Don't worry about it. It's an old shirt."

"It still has plenty of wear left in it. There's no reason to ruin it."

"I'll take care of it after you're done with it."

She looked around as if she were trying to decide what to do next.

""Would you like a drink?" she offered. "There's some beer in the refrigerator and some bottles on top of the cabinet. Help yourself."

"I'll have a beer. Would you like something?"

"I'd love a brandy."

He went into the kitchen and poured the drinks. By the time he returned, she had taken off his shirt and put on an old dressing gown. He handed her the brandy.

"Thanks," she said. "Your shirt is soaking in the bathroom sink. I'll wash it for you."

"You didn't have to do that, you know."

"I may be helpless, but I'm not quite useless."

"I'm worried about leaving you here alone."

"I'll be all right. I have everything I need here. And I can always call you to come galloping to my rescue if something comes up—provided you write down your phone number."

"Is there anything else you want me to do before I leave?"

"I'd really like to take a bath. I think I can manage, but I'd appreciate it if you would stand by in case I need help."

"I'll bathe you if you like."

She smiled. "Thanks for the offer, but I should try to preserve some aura of mystery. I'll let you run my bath water, though, if you would be so kind."

"Anything to oblige, ma'am," he said with a fake western drawl.

After they had finished their drinks, he ran the tub half full of water, then helped himself to another beer while she took a bath. She managed to get the job done without his assistance, which disappointed him a little.

As he waited for her to finish her bath, he looked around her apartment. It appeared to be a little more expensive than his. Her choice of decorations was also more tasteful than his. She had some art work on the walls while he had less expensive copies and photos. The books on the shelves were fewer in number, but they reflected good taste and a wide range of interest. She had tapes rather than records, and he was not able to read the labels from his vantage point across the room. There were no photographs on display. There was an assortment of magazines on the coffee table, of which a current issue of <u>Time</u> was evident. It occurred to him that he could easily find out her real name by simply looking at the mailing label on one of the magazines, but he deliberately chose not to do so.

After about half an hour she came out of the bathroom. "Thank you for waiting," she said. "I feel a lot better now. I'm sure I'll sleep better tonight."

"That's good. Will you call me in the morning?"

"Why don't you come here for lunch? I owe you at least two meals."

"Do you think you'll be up to fixing lunch?"

"I'll have to fix something for myself anyway. Besides, I don't plan to lie around in bed waiting for this thing to heal."

"Good. I'll see you tomorrow then."

He gave her a kiss, taking care not to do anything to put

pressure on the wound. She returned his kiss as if it were a totally natural response. Then he walked downstairs to his car and drove away.

"What are you getting yourself into now?" he thought. He turned on the radio and recognized the strains of Mahler's <u>First Symphony</u>.

The next morning Wagner got up at seven, put on his sweat suit, and ran along the lake for nearly an hour. The temperature was gradually rising with the advance of spring. He was pleased to notice that his physical condition had not deteriorated appreciably during his sojourn as a shoe salesman. He returned to his apartment, showered, ate breakfast, and looked through his mail. He re-read the letter from the department which offered him back his old job. He telephoned his supervisor, Lieutenant Gerhardt, and arranged to return to work the following Monday. The lieutenant sounded quite non-committal about the entire arrangement, but he always sounded like that. After talking to Gerhardt, Wagner wondered just what his new arrangement with Judge Carrol and Company would be. He supposed that he would find out soon enough.

At eleven-thirty he left for Sylvia's apartment. He knocked on her door at three minutes before the hour. After some delay, she answered the door. She had made an effort to fix her hair and apply make-up, but the effects of the ordeal still showed on her face. Nevertheless, she smiled and seemed glad to see him. She was wearing slacks and a thin light-blue blouse. As she moved between Wagner and the window and stood sideways to him, he could see through the blouse. The sight disturbed him and reminded him of the adage that a woman partly dressed is sexier than one totally naked. He couldn't deny the truth of it. With that in the forefront of his mind, he asked, "How's your chest today?"

She grinned at him. "Now what kind of a question is that to ask of a lady?"

"Begging the lady's pardon," he said with an affected British accent, "But I merely wished to inquire as to the status of Madame's right mammary."

"Well, if the gentleman must know," she said in the same mock dialect, "It's healing nicely, thank you."

"And did Milady enjoy a pleasant night's repose?"

"Tolerable, kind sir. But Milady would have been better advised not to mix brandy with medicine."

"Ah, yes. I wondered about that at the time."

"It probably didn't hurt anything, but I was kept awake by the rumbling of my stomach until midnight."

"You seem to be moving better today."

"Some of the soreness is gone, but I really notice it if I bend or squat down and then stand up too quickly."

"Then we'd better not play leap-frog this afternoon."

"That's really thoughtful of you."

He took a deep breath. "I smell our lunch cooking. Can I help you with anything?"

"You can pour the coffee while I serve the casserole."

"You shouldn't have gone to so much trouble."

"No trouble. It was frozen."

"Good show. What do you suppose people did before freezers were invented?"

"They probably went out for pizza a lot."

"I never thought of that possibility."

"I wonder why not."

They ate their meal in silence, then relaxed with a second cup of coffee. Sylvia looked thoughtful for a moment and said, "I heard from our mutual friend this morning. Did you?"

"No."

"I didn't think so. He asked me to pass along some information to you. I'm to be your contact now."

Wagner looked surprised, but didn't say anything. He thought, "So this is how they want to handle our compromised identities."

"I'm to work at the Cook County Bureau of Public Records. That way I'll have access to information about a lot of people who are of interest to the organization. They want you to pass on information concerning criminal activity outside police jurisdiction. That is, activity outside Chicago itself as well as situations which the police can't touch for one reason or another."

"That sounds like organized crime again. I wonder just how far they're prepared to go with this."

"I don't know. Maybe the question should be how far we are prepared to go along with them."

Wagner thought for a moment, then said, "I could show you a mansion outside Lake Forest just north of here. The man who lives there has his hands in more illegal enterprises than you can imagine, and that has been common knowledge for at least fifteen years. TV crews take pictures of him and his family going to church on Sunday morning. His wife sends him off to work every weekday morning as if he were any other business man. He has a whole law firm figuring out how to move his money into dummy corporations so he can stay one step ahead of the IRS and other government investigators."

"What's his name? Corleone?"

"No. Vickers."

"Do you think I should mention him to my contact?"

"Not unless you want to be laughed at. That would be like telling them that Mayor Daley is a Democrat. Vickers is one of the four or five most powerful men in the Midwest."

"Then why are you telling me about him?"

"Because it's the existence of people like him who motivate

me to stay with this. Some people are beyond the law. Now we have a means to deal with their ilk because we've also put ourselves beyond the law."

"Doesn't it bother you that we killed two men this week?"

He didn't answer immediately, but then said, "Let me try to give you an analogy. When I was fourteen or fifteen, I spent part of a summer on a sheep ranch in Wyoming. While I was there helping the herder, a pack of stray dogs attacked the flock and went after the lambs. The herder didn't waste any time trying to find out if anybody owned the dogs. He just shot them. I must have looked pretty upset about that, so he offered me a brief rationale: 'What else are you gonna do with killer dogs?' After several years of police work, I've come to a similar conclusion: What else are you going to do with people who prey on the most vulnerable victims they can find? Nothing has worked. The problem keeps getting worse. There are dozens more like Scales and Hulsman out there, and nothing we can do will change them. They're just like the wild dogs that attack lambs. No, I don't feel any remorse for killing them, especially when the legal system can't even imprison them. If that seems callous, I'm sorry, but that's the way I feel."

"You don't have to apologize to me. After all, I helped you do it. I can't say that I'd care to get that close to the action again, though. I'm in basic sympathy for your sentiments, but I'd rather remain more detached from the front lines. Maybe I'm a coward at heart."

"The lady who jumped on Hulsman's back was no coward. The engraving on your chest is proof of that."

"Just the same, I'd prefer to leave the heroics to the men. My notion of feminine equality doesn't extend that far."

"Well, I'm glad we're still working together. I'd take you as a partner any time."

"You'd better be careful what you're saying," she said with a grin.

"You know what I mean."

"Yes, I do, and I appreciate the compliment."

Wagner couldn't think of an immediate response, so changed the subject. "I have to start work at the department again next week. When do you begin your new job?"

"As soon as I'm functional. Probably also some time next week."

"Would you like to do something this weekend?"

"Sure," she replied. "If I'm still not up and about, you can come here."

"That's fine. If it's nice and you feel up to it, we might take a run up to Wisconsin. Otherwise, we'll stay here and I'll tell you the story of my life."

"In two hundred words or less," she teased.

Wagner stayed until about six. By then it was apparent that Sylvia was experiencing more discomfort, even though she tried not to show it. He insisted that she lie down for a while and rest. She complied reluctantly and promptly fell asleep. Wagner washed the dishes, straightened up the kitchen, and put everything away. Then he looked in on Sylvia again and saw that she was sleeping soundly. For the life of him, he couldn't picture her getting into a fight with anyone, let alone taking on a goon from the protection racket. It was fortunate for him that she had, though.

"I still think you're quite a woman," he said softly, knowing that she couldn't hear him. "Thanks for the meal."

Then he left the apartment, locking the door behind him.

9

The next Monday Wagner ended his enforced absence from the police force. He stopped by Lieutenant Gerhardt's office first, but the latter was out for the morning. Next he had to visit several other offices in the headquarters building to take care of the administrative aspects of his reinstatement. No one seemed particularly concerned about either his unusual absence or his return to duty. Everyone processed him in a matter-of-fact manner. Wagner wondered just what strings had been pulled to cause his suspension to be lifted. By the time he had finished processing, he still had no idea.

After picking up his badge and identification card, he went to his old office. As he opened the door, he encountered the first reception of the day that was more than perfunctory.

"The prodigal son is back! Kill the fatted calf!" roared the big man behind the desk. It was Fletcher, his partner of three years.

"Hello, Fletch," said Wagner, feeling a little gratified by the boisterous welcome.

Fletcher engulfed Wagner's hand in a huge paw and gripped it hard enough to make him wince.

"I just heard about it yesterday," said the big man. "What the hell happened anyway?"

Wagner shrugged. "You know how it is when you're indispensable. The department just couldn't function without me, so they begged me to come back to save you poor slobs from total chaos."

Fletcher roared with laughter, never suspecting the evasiveness of Wagner's answer.

"I tried to call you several times, but you were never home," said Fletcher.

"I haven't been home much lately. Staying in the apartment gets old in a hurry."

` "Yeah, I'll bet it does. Especially when you're used to moving around a lot."

It would not have occurred to Fletcher to ask Wagner what he had been doing. Their friendship was reserved almost exclusively for duty hours. That was probably due to the fact that, aside from their work, they had remarkably little in common.

"What are you up to these days?" Wagner asked.

"We've been trying to chase down a welfare scam on the South Side. Not far from Rosie's place, actually. It seems that some enterprising soul has gone into the free-lance banking business. Someone is buying food stamps and cashing welfare checks at a fraction of their face value with no questions asked. No ID, no nothin'. And they're not a bit fussy about where the checks come from."

It took Wagner just a few seconds to calculate the implications of such a scheme.

"Wonderful!" he exclaimed sarcastically. "That means that the people on welfare have to stand by their mailboxes with clubs to keep from getting ripped off."

"And then go right out, cash the check, and pay the bills," continued Fletcher.

"Because with this friendly neighborhood banking service, every petty thief in the area will be following the mailmen," Wagner completed.

"You get the picture."

"So we have to follow the people who follow the mailmen and persuade one of them to tell us who is cashing the checks."

"We've tried that. That's how we know what we do about

the set-up. But the guy wouldn't tell us where the bank is located. Said he was afraid of what the higher-ups might do to him. So we brought in some more suspects. Read them their rights. They wouldn't talk. We had no reason to hold them. We let them go. Back to square one."

"Fletch, have you ever considered the psychology of persuasion?"

"Come on, Wagner. You just lost your badge with your powers of persuasion. There has to be another way."

"How long have you been working on this operation?"

"Off and on for about three weeks."

"You'll get old and gray waiting for somebody to lead you by the hand to the bankers."

"At least I'll be able to retire that way. Besides, maybe we'll get lucky one of these days."

"While you're waiting to get lucky, maybe you'll look the other way while I try to improve our luck."

Fletcher looked at him sadly and shook his head. "I used to think they made us partners because I was big enough to take care of you and you were smart enough to do the same for me. Now you don't seem to need my help anymore, and I'm not so sure about how smart you are. You didn't used to take chances when you didn't have to."

"If you don't take a few risks, you don't get many results."

"What's happened to you, Wagner? You act like you're fighting a war out there. Most of us are just doing a job, you know. And not even a very well-paying one at that."

Wagner mulled that over for a minute. Then he said, "Stick with me, Fletch. There's nobody I'd rather work with. And I promise not to get your head on a block."

Fletcher grinned. "Actually it was a part at the other end of my anatomy that I was worried about."

As Wagner laughed, he rapidly thought of several tight

situations when he and Fletcher had used their combined resources to come out intact. One night two years earlier they had tried to arrest a robbery suspect in a bar only to have six or seven angry friends of the man attack them. Fletcher had assumed the protective role and fought like a man possessed. Wagner could think of no one else who could have handled odds like that. Out of such situations had grown a bond that transcended friendship.

But the business at hand seemed unlikely to put them in any such situation. It was just a dull piece of detective work that was more likely to be boring than dangerous or exciting.

"When are the welfare checks delivered next?" Wagner asked.

"Some should be out tomorrow."

"Let's tag along behind a postal vehicle and see what we can see. Today we can talk to some people who've lost their checks and see if they can tell us anything."

And so they began a long, tedious process in hopes of turning up some scrap of useful information. The questioning process produced no results. They never expected that it would. The two partners followed a mailman at a distance all that week, but nothing happened. Saturday morning they followed a different letter carrier for three hours, but saw no one who appeared interested in the deliveries other than the people who had a legitimate concern. They checked with two other teams, but the others had fared no better.

Wagner went home at noon with a deep sense of frustration. During the previous month he had operated outside the law and gotten immediate results. Now he was working within the scope of the system and was spinning his wheels.

After eating lunch and changing clothes, he picked up Sylvia and took her for a drive. She was feeling better and said that the cut was healing nicely. She expected to start work the following Monday. Wagner made an immodest reference to the success of his medical efforts, to which she replied, "I'd better not compliment you too much. I'll have you offering to take care of all my medical needs."

"What's wrong with that?" he asked. "How many doctors do you know who make house calls?"

They drove northward toward Wisconsin by way of the lake country, one of the few regions of Illinois which could be called scenic by anyone who had been farther away than Iowa. The radio was playing a selection from a recent Mozart festival.

"How does it feel to be back on the force?" she asked.

He thought for a moment before answering. "Good in some ways. I like working with Fletcher. He isn't as good-looking as you, but other than that he's as good a partner as I could ask for. There's also more of a sense of security in working for an established organization. You know. Pension, health insurance, fringe benefits. That sort of thing. But it sure is frustrating trying to solve a case by pick-and-shovel work. Then we don't even know whether anyone will follow through if and when we solve it."

Sylvia was quiet for a while as she mulled over his comments. Then she said, "You know, working with you has really destroyed any notion I may have had about police stereotypes."

"You mean we're not all Boston Blackies and Dirty Harrys?"

"Not even Inspector Clouseaus," she said with a grin.

"Shucks! I always thought Hollywood was just itching to do my life story."

"No, seriously, just compare yourself and Fletcher. He's the big cop who can make his presence felt just by his size and strength. At least, that's what you've told me."

"Except that he hardly ever does that. He's actually pretty gentle, if the truth were known."

"So are you, as I've found out. But where he can intimidate

people by his size, when he has to, you take care of yourself by mental discipline and a lot of physical conditioning."

Wagner shrugged. "Something like that, I guess."

"And neither of you is very much like the policeman image that most of us have picked up from fiction."

"That's probably to our credit. Cops are just people. We don't fit into neat categories any better than the rest of you folks."

They continued to chat amiably and enjoy a warm, sunny spring day. The afternoon passed quickly. They ate supper along the way, and Wagner took her home fairly early.

The next week Wagner and Fletcher went back to work on the check-cashing operation. The first two days went by with no results. More checks were reported stolen, but the investigating officers were unable to find out anything about the circumstances.

Finally a break came in an unexpected manner. They were following a mailman on foot when they noticed a scuffle in the hallway of an old apartment house. They rushed in and found a young man lying on the floor surrounded by three women and two old men. All five had sticks or canes and were beating the young man. Even when Fletcher identified himself as a police officer, they were reluctant to back off.

"We caught him goin' through the mail boxes," said a shrill-voiced woman. "He's the one been stealin' our checks."

The young man was too dazed to respond. He had been badly beaten, and his head was bloody.

Wagner squatted down beside the fallen man. "What do you have to say for yourself?" he asked.

The young man looked puzzled. "Ain't you gonna read me

my rights? I don't have to say nothin'. I was jus' checkin' the mail when these folks unloaded on me."

"He don't even live in this neighborhood," yelled one of the women.

Fletcher held the angry group back while Wagner continued to talk to the accused thief.

"I'm not going to read you your rights," he said quietly. "I'm going to ask you a question, and if you don't answer, my partner and I are going to walk away from here. You got it?"

The young man looked panicky as he eyed the group of enraged tenants. "You can't do that," he protested.

"Then suppose you tell me who cashes welfare checks with no identification."

The young man's eyes grew large with fright. "Man, they'd kill me if I tol' you that."

"You have about fifteen seconds to decide."

The beaten man was faced with a terrible dilemma, and his head injury did not contribute toward a rational appraisal of the situation.

After a few seconds, Wagner stood up and motioned for Fletcher to allow the group to advance a few feet.

"I'll tell you!" screamed the man. "Just get me out of here!"

"Tell me now!" Wagner said menacingly.

The man gave an address, and Wagner wrote it down. Then he took out a worn card from his pocket and intoned: "You have the right to remain silent. Anything you say..."

Fletcher called for a police ambulance, then sent out an assembly call for the other two teams in the area. Wagner stayed with the thief until the ambulance arrived, then joined Fletcher to wait for the other teams.

"What did you say to him?" asked Fletcher. "I can't believe you got him to talk without laying a hand on him."

"I told him that unless he cooperated, I'd put out the word

on the block that he got beat up by a little old lady on roller skates."

Before he could answer the question seriously, the other two cars arrived. All six men gathered at Wagner and Fletcher's car, where Wagner explained what had happened.

"We have an address for the bankers, but we need to hit it fast. If they get word of this bust, they'll be gone before we ever get there."

Wagner outlined a hasty plan, and they all left within two minutes. Since all the cars were unmarked, they drove casually to three different spots near the address. One team moved to the back of the building, a second stayed out front, and Wagner and Fletcher went to the front door. The partners were painfully aware that they had no warrant for search or arrest.

The building in question appeared to be a non-descript business office of some kind. There was no sign to identify it and nothing in the window to give a clue as to what kind of business was transacted there. As the two policemen entered, a man looked up from his desk. His expression was not exactly poised, but he asked calmly, "What can I do for you gentlemen?"

"I'd like to see your stock of wallpaper," said Wagner.

The man looked totally puzzled. "I think you've made a mistake," he said. "We don't handle wallpaper here."

"That's funny," said Wagner. "I distinctly heard a man in the hospital say you handled paper here."

While the man struggled to maintain his composure, there was a shuffling noise in the other room. Someone was running out the back. The man at the desk stood up and looked undecided for a moment, as if he were trying to decide whether to run also. He decided not to.

"I don't know anything. I just work here," he said at last.

"Why don't you step outside with us?" Wagner invited.

The man put on his coat. As he left the building, Wagner

said, "You're under arrest for suspicion of receiving stolen goods. Anything you say..."

The team covering the rear caught two men running out the back door. Wagner instructed the others to take all three suspects to police headquarters. He had the second team guard the building while he called in a request for a search warrant. They would at least conduct that part of the operation according to standard procedure.

The search turned up ample evidence of the suspected check-cashing operation. Numerous welfare checks showed signatures with remarkably similar handwriting. They also found a large supply of food stamps and several thousand dollars in cash.

Fletcher shook his head. "It's too bad we can't sit here and greet every punk who comes in to cash his stolen checks and food stamps. We'd have a field day if we could keep the bust a secret. But the word gets around fast. Only the village idiot would show up after all this commotion."

"Don't worry," said Wagner. "By tomorrow somebody else will have figured out how and where to set up another bank."

"What a jungle! Imagine trying to get rich by ripping off poor people."

"That's what we call the Reverse Robin Hood Syndrome," quipped Wagner. "You steal from the poor and give to the rich."

"Well, at least we put this operation out of business."

"Sure. Thanks to some women and old men who got fed up with all this crap and turned on the sharks. If it hadn't been for them, we'd be following the mail until the cows come home."

"So we got a break. Don't knock it. Come on and let me buy you a beer."

"That's easily the best idea you've had all day."

10

Sylvia had invited Wagner to supper that night. He arrived at her apartment just before seven. She seemed to have everything ready by the time he arrived. She was wearing a pretty red dress and appeared to be fully recovered from her recent wound.

"You look pretty sharp," he remarked. "You're moving well, too. Just as good as new, aren't you?"

"Thank you, sir. I feel just fine. You won't have to help me to the bathroom or anything."

"How's your new job coming?" he asked, unable to think of a witty response to her last remark.

"It looks as if it might be fairly interesting. I've been visiting other Cook County facilities to get an overview of the administrative system. It occurred to me that there must be entire states that don't have this elaborate a set-up."

"That would figure. Cook County has a bigger population than a lot of states."

"Yesterday I learned one rather gruesome statistic. We visited the county morgue. The guide said that every Saturday night they expect to get six to ten homicide victims. Most of them are poor minorities who get in fights, usually after drinking too much. I suppose you know about all that, but I didn't. It really bothered me."

"Not exactly the Agatha Christie type of victim, are they? Someone files a one-page report. Unless someone complains, there isn't even much of an attempt made to find out who killed them. There are just too many."

"How utterly depressing!"

"Now you can see why someone in my line of work gets a little cynical about something called the 'right to life.' In every culture there are certain people who live just a narrow margin away from death. Some have a precarious food supply. Some never know what clean water is. Others have nasty neighbors. Here we are in the middle of the richest nation in world history, and we still have people who live in those situations. What does the right to life mean to them?"

"I guess I never thought about it in that light."

"We hold these truths to be self-evident, that all men are created equal, that they are endowed by their Creator with certain inalienable rights, that among these rights are life…"

"…liberty, and the pursuit of happiness. The Declaration of Independence."

"There's your right to life. A fine bit of idealism. But just what does it mean in real terms?" he asked.

She thought for a moment. "In practical terms, I'd say that it means that if you can get enough to eat and persuade your neighbor not to do you in, you have the right to live until you die of something other than starvation or violence."

He chuckled humorlessly. "And I thought I was getting cynical."

"Maybe we both are, at least a little. But we are also trying to do something to change things."

"I wonder. Are we accomplishing anything? Sometimes I feel like Sisyphus in Greek mythology. It was his fate to roll a boulder up a hill so that he could keep chasing it back down the hill and roll it back up again. The same thing over and over."

"At least we have to give him credit for determination and persistence."

"So we do. Say, this is a lot of heavy conversation on an empty stomach."

"You're right. Supper should be ready. It's all in the oven. We're having stuffed green peppers and baked potatoes."

"Sounds great!"

Wagner opened a bottle of Riesling wine while Sylvia put their supper on the table. He waited to tell her about the conclusion of the banking operation until she asked. As usual, he needed some coaxing before he would discuss his work. She was interested in the details, though, and was quick to pick up on the irony of the fact that some of the victims had been instrumental in solving the case.

"It sounds as if you operate in nearly as unorthodox a manner as you did when you were with our group," she observed. "Do you always play it that loose with the rules?"

"I used to think of myself as pretty four-square. Everybody bends the rules a little now and then, but I generally tried to play it pretty straight. Maybe my stint with you and your friends changed my perspective just a bit."

"Just don't get careless and find yourself in trouble again."

"Yes, Mother."

"OK, I asked for that."

"No, you didn't. It was a cheap shot, and I'm sorry I said that. Actually I'm pleased to have you care enough to be concerned."

"Surely someone else must be concerned about you. Are your parents still living?"

"No, they died when the planet Krypton exploded. I was raised by an old couple in Kansas who..."

"All right. I should have known. You've been serious for at least twenty minutes."

"I'm always serious. It's just that sometimes I'm more serious than other times."

"Even when you're Superman?"

"Don't say it so loud!" he protested in mock alarm. "It's a secret."

"Oh, I forgot. Had you considered that my real name might be Lois Lane?"

"Can't be. I used my x-ray vision to read the tags on your underwear."

She crossed her arms across her breasts in feigned embarrassment.

"It's too late for that. I've already seen them. Remember?"

"How can I forget? You remind me about it at every opportunity."

"Must have made a big impression."

"Why don't we have some dessert?" she asked, deliberately changing the subject. "I baked a chocolate cake."

"Terrific! If you'd eaten at my place, you'd have gotten half of an orange popsicle."

"Don't you ever try to bake?"

"Not if I can help it. I'm the only one I know who can mess up a Betty Crocker cake mix."

"It doesn't sound as if you put much effort into cooking."

"It's actually part of my diet plan. I fix everything so badly that it kills my appetite just to look at it."

They ate their dessert, made small talk as they drank their coffee, cleared the table, and retired to the living room.

"That was an excellent meal," he said. "Now it's my turn to treat you again. How about tomorrow night?"

"Only if you promise not to cook."

"I could have it catered. There's a Kosher delicatessen near my place."

"That would be fine. Or a pizza. You never did take me out for a pizza like you promised."

"How about a Jewish pizza?"

"Oy vey! With lox instead of anchovies."

"Or maybe gefillte fish wrapped in pizza dough and cut to look like a bagel."

She laughed. "For a guy who can't fry a decent hamburger, you sure have a vivid imagination for food."

"I'm basically a supervisor. I excel at watching other people work."

"Well, while we're on the subject of supervision, I have something from our mutual friend that requests your professional opinion. Maybe we can take care of that before I forget about it."

"OK. Let's have it."

"It has to do with organized crime. As I understand it, there are several groups operating in and around Chicago. Some of them cooperate with one or more of the other groups. Others are independent and compete with rival gangs. They range in size from a handful of members to those with contacts all over the world. How am I doing so far?"

"Pretty basic, but on target," he replied.

"We've tangled with some of the smaller fish in these organizations, such as our late and unlamented friends from the protection business. The top men are pretty well beyond reach. They can afford the best legal counsel. Some have the best security guards and systems available. They usually channel their money into legitimate enterprises to cover their sources from the rackets. Even when their identities are known, those at the top are usually immune from prosecution."

"Right. I told you about Mr. Vickers up in Lake Forest. I've known ever since I started here that he was into drugs, gambling, loan sharking, and prostitution. That's as far as it goes. He hasn't even been arrested lately."

"OK. Here's the 64-dollar question: How would you go about reaching somebody like him?"

Wagner just looked at her for a minute. "You mean, how do you touch the untouchables?"

"That's right."

"Well, you could rent an airplane and drop a bomb on his house. That's considered tacky in some circles, though."

"Admittedly. Try again."

"Over the years there have only been two effective ways of reaching people like that…with any degree of consistency, that is. One is for the IRS to get after them for income tax evasion. That used to work sometimes. The feds even got Al Capone that way. The other way is for a rival mob to get some big ideas. People in the mobs are much more effective at exterminating each other than any police agency ever could. That's because they aren't as restricted in their methods. They've actually done a pretty good job on each other. There have been over a thousand gangland homicides since anyone bothered to keep score."

"How could we apply that to our form of operation?"

Wagner was silent for a minute while he thought about the problem. "Suppose we were to zero in on the heads of two mobs that didn't like each other very much to start with. Let's say we find a couple of second-rate hoods and hire them to fill a contract on the big-shots. There are plenty of losers out there who would kill somebody for $2,500 or less. So they try it, and unless they get extremely lucky, they fail. Instead they get caught by the chief's strong-arm associates. In the course of the ensuing discussion, it comes to light that they heard the name of the rival gang mentioned during the initial briefing."

"And in the fracas that follows, there's no telling how many might meet with an untimely demise."

Wagner shrugged. "I didn't say it was pretty or tidy. You just asked how it might be done. In effect, it would mean trying to start a gang war."

"I'll pass that on to my contact."

"It isn't a very novel idea. I'm sure they've already thought about something like that. I wonder if they're after somebody in particular or are just gathering ideas for future reference."

"I have a notion that they're after somebody specific, but I don't know for sure."

"Well, if they're looking for a nominating committee, I'm available. Earlier we were talking about people who live on the underside of the poverty level. Can you imagine that a lot of people get rich by raking in what little money those people have?"

"Why pick on the poor?" she asked.

"Because they're an easy target. Lots of them are poor because they're ignorant. Or the other way around. Either way, poverty and ignorance seem to go together. When you're poor and hopeless, you're more likely to blow your last few bucks on something to take your mind off your troubles. Some buy cheap booze. Some buy drugs. Others rent a warm body to sleep with. Then when the money is gone, lots of them borrow at high interest rates to carry them until the next payday or welfare check. And the mobsters are out there cashing in on all that human misery."

Sylvia held her head in her hands for a minute, then said, "It really stinks, doesn't it?"

"That it does."

"Do you think there's a solution to it all, Richard?"

"I don't really know. Maybe in time. It has to start with somebody caring, though. I don't know how to justify what we're doing about this, but at least we're doing something. Too many people are just throwing up their hands and saying it's hopeless."

She put her arms around him. "Then let's stay with it. We might both wind up in jail, but at least we will have tried to do something."

"Lady, did anyone ever tell you that you have a very persuasive manner?"

11

The next morning as Wagner read the <u>Chicago Tribune</u> he noticed an obscure article with the heading, "Police Puzzled by Disappearances." With a strange sense of foreboding, he read the article:

"A spokesman for the Chicago Police Department has denied any knowledge concerning the disappearances of Harold McMorrow and Cecil Forbes. McMorrow, age 29, was released last Wednesday from the state penitentiary at Joliet. He had been serving four years and two months of a fifteen-year sentence for armed robbery and assault with a deadly weapon. His father, William R. McMorrow of Chicago, reported that the younger McMorrow had left Joliet by bus Wednesday, but never reached home. He was due to report to his parole officer on Friday, but failed to do so. A prison spokesman confirmed the fact that McMorrow had boarded the bus for Chicago.

"Forbes, age 41, was last seen immediately after his acquittal in municipal court last Tuesday. The much-publicized case involved the alleged assault and rape of two teen-aged girls near Circle Campus last December. After his acquittal, Forbes went out to celebrate with some friends. One of them, Walter George, said that they had arranged to meet at a specified bar, but that Forbes never showed up. None of his friends or relatives claims to have seen him since that time. The police are investigating the possibility of foul play."

Wagner read the article a second time. It occurred to him that if he were to make an educated guess, he would bet that McMorrow had changed buses and headed for parts unknown, and that Forbes would be found in an alley with his ribs kicked in. And if he were to make a second guess, he would stick to his original assessment of McMorrow's situation and revise his theory on Forbes to allow for the possibility of an abduction to a crematorium in the western suburbs. It would be interesting to see if a follow-up article appeared.

Wagner stared at the last sentence of the article: "The police are investigating the possibility of foul play." That line struck him as highly ironic. What comprises foul play? Ostensibly it involved someone interfering with the freedom of a person who had been released by a responsible agency of the law. But what if the person being released still constituted a significant threat to others? Wasn't it "foul play" to turn such a person loose? Wagner thought of his analogy of the wild dogs and the sheep and found that he had very little concern for the welfare of Mr. McMorrow or Mr. Forbes.

Looking at the clock, he saw that he had very little time left to contemplate the mysteries of the universe. He just had time to finish his coffee, put on his tie, and leave for work.

He arrived at headquarters with two minutes to spare. Fletcher was already there working on the report of their last case. His two-fingered technique on the typewriter was almost as fast as his printing with a blunt pencil. Either way, he managed to misspell every third word.

"How do you spell 'illicit'?" he asked as Wagner came in.

"Two L's," replied Wagner.

"I know that. How many I's?"

"Why don't you just fake it and let one of the secretaries clean it up?"

"Good idea. Better yet, why don't you do this? You can type a lot faster than I can."

"Is that all we have lined up today?"

"Nope. As soon as we finish this report, we have a briefing upstairs. Gerhardt has something for us."

"Doesn't he know it's Friday? He wouldn't do anything to screw up our weekend, would he?"

Fletcher gave him a funny look. "What happened to your sense of dedication? How do you expect to make America safe for democracy if you worry about such a trivial matter as a weekend?"

"Well, actually I was looking forward to reading the book of regulations just to make sure that I hadn't missed anything while I was out of contact."

"I should have known better. Please forgive me for doubting your sense of dedication, o noble one!"

"I'll think about it and let you know next week."

"How magnanimous of you!"

"True," said Wagner magnanimously, then both of them started laughing. "You know, three years ago you were a no-nonsense sort of guy. Now you talk just as crazy as I do."

"That's what my wife says. I always blame it on you."

"Here," said Wagner wiping his eyes, "Let me take a crack at that typewriter, and we'll hammer out this report."

Working together, the two men finished the report before noon and took an early lunch break. They were back by one o'clock and reported to their superior, Lieutenant Gerhardt. Wagner had only seen Gerhardt briefly since his return to duty, so he was uncertain as to how the lieutenant felt about his reinstatement. As it turned out, Gerhardt was all business and gave no indication of his attitude toward Wagner. The beginning of the briefing was somewhat misleading, though.

"How would you two like to go fishing next week?" he asked.

Neither Wagner nor Fletcher had a quick answer for that.

"I'm serious. We have an eighteen-foot Starcraft with a 55 horsepower Evinrude engine. I want you to be at Calumet Harbor at seven o'clock next Monday to go fishing. The

Coho salmon are running. You can buy your own lures this weekend."

The two partners maintained matching sober expressions. Neither was willing to ask the obvious question: "What's the catch?" The lieutenant continued the mystery until he was sure that neither would ask it. Finally he broke the suspense himself.

"I suppose you're wondering why I'm assigning you to go fishing."

"No," replied Fletcher with a straight face. "We just do as we're told."

Gerhardt chose to ignore the remark. "We're watching members of the Koster organization. We received a tip that a planeload of heroin was diverted from Chicago to Milwaukee due to fog here, and they want to move it down. They know they're under heavy surveillance up there, and the tip says they plan to use their vehicles as decoys while they move the stuff by boat. The lake has been rough this week, but it's supposed to calm down next week. We've identified two cabin cruisers at the marina here as belonging to Koster. I have pictures of them. Your job will be to troll back and forth along with the thousand or so fishing nuts and try to find out what they're doing. Newman and Day will be in another boat. You'll be in radio contact with them and with us here."

"So we're going fishing as a cover for the fact that what we're really doing is going fishing," Fletcher commented.

"You might look at it that way," replied the lieutenant dryly. "Get receipts for your fishing licenses and any tackle you need. There'll be rods and reels in the boat."

"Any idea how long we'll be doing this?" Wagner asked.

"That depends on what you see. You could be weathered out, too. At the most, it won't be more than two weeks or so. The salmon move north as the lake warms. We don't want you to be the only fishermen left on this end of the lake. Besides, let's think positive. Maybe you'll see something. We also have the Coast Guard ready to back you up if you need them."

Gerhardt finished the briefing, and the two partners went out to buy the necessary equipment for the next week. They bought a variety of trolling lures, a large landing net, and some warm rubberized gloves.

"We'd better get a big ice chest, too," said Fletcher.

"Do you think we'll catch that many fish?"

"Who cares about fish? This is for beer."

"Since when do we drink beer on duty?" asked Wagner.

"It's part of our cover. We're supposed to look like fishermen, aren't we?"

"Well, in that case I suppose we could make an exception to policy."

"Consider it a sacrifice for the greater cause."

"What are we sacrificing?"

"Our principles! What else?"

"Oh, those. Well, it weighs heavily upon my conscience, but when you put it in those terms, I suppose I'll have to relent just this once."

Fletcher grinned at the put-on. "I never thought I'd have to go to so much trouble to convince a German to drink beer."

They finished their shopping, turned in the receipts for reimbursement, and parted company for the weekend. Although the two men were good friends, they rarely socialized together. That was partly because Wagner didn't care much for Fletcher's wife, who was a shrill, complaining woman. If the truth were known, Fletcher didn't especially care for her either, but he dutifully went home to her every night and listened to her list of grievances.

After work, Wagner went back to his apartment. He just had time to take a shower and change clothes before it was time to pick up Sylvia for supper. He had decided to make good his threat to take her out for pizza.

When he reached her apartment, she was still getting ready to go out. On the coffee table were a scrap book and several newspaper clippings. He scanned the articles quickly and recognized two of them from the <u>Tribune</u>. One was about a six-year-old girl who had hit another little girl in the face with a stick. The attorney for the victim's parents was demanding that the six-year-old be tried as an adult for battery. Embarrassed officials were hoping that the two sets of parents could work out a solution, but no compromise had been reached by that time.

"That's pretty good," thought Wagner. "A fifteen year-old kills somebody and gets juvenile detention. A six-year-old gets in a fight and suddenly becomes an adult."

The next article was about a woman in Chicago who was beaten by a man who had been convicted of several violent crimes. The police caught the man and persuaded the woman to testify against him. She agreed to do so. The man was then released on $100 bail, but the police refused to provide her with protection. She lived in constant fear of reprisal until the man was arrested again for a sex crime. The man was offered release on bail again, but this time was unable to raise the amount. He went to trial. The woman testified against him. He was convicted, but after a round of plea bargaining, he was sentenced to seven months in jail. The woman, her confidence shattered, swore to sleep with a butcher knife on the night stand.

Wagner shook his head as he dropped the clipping and picked up the next one. It was a magazine article about Terre Haute, Indiana, where the police chief had declared war on people who commit armed robbery. He had given his patrolmen instructions to take drastic action to halt such crimes. His unusual approach to law enforcement had produced three results: It had incurred the wrath of the American Civil Liberties Union. It had reduced the incidence of violent crime by forty-three percent. And it had resulted in no shots fired by the police.

That was as far as Wagner had gotten when Sylvia reappeared. Wagner looked up and smiled.

"Hello again," he said. "You're looking right sharp this evening."

"Thank you, kind sir," she replied.

"I've been looking at your newspaper clippings. What are you doing?"

"I started keeping a collection of articles about the peculiarities of our legal system. I don't think it will take me very long to fill that scrap book."

"Is this part of your work, or are you just doing it for the fun of it?"

"It isn't part of my job, and it's hardly what you would call fun. I suppose I'm doing it to reinforce my motives for working outside the system."

"Do you really need that kind of reinforcement?"

"Sometimes. Don't you still have doubts about it now and then?"

"I suppose so, but I also have something else to keep me going."

"What's that?"

"Trying to work within the system."

"Really?"

"You bet. Right now we're trying to intercept a big drug shipment. We know who is doing it and how they're doing it, but we have to catch them actually in the act."

"Do you expect to catch them?"

Wagner shrugged. "Who knows?"

Sylvia frowned. "Did you read the article about the Terre Haute police chief?"

"Yes. It's interesting to see what happens when someone puts some teeth into the system."

"But the Civil Liberties Union is fighting his approach. Do you think they can force a change of policy?"

"Probably. They think that the Constitution guarantees us an equal right to get mugged."

"Wasn't that the organization that defended the right of the American Nazi Party to have a parade in a predominantly Jewish community?"

"Skokie. They proved their point, too. The only reason there was no parade was because the Nazis backed down. You talk about a nightmare for the police!"

"What are they trying to prove? The ACLU, I mean."

"I suppose they're just trying to carry all of our constitutional freedoms to their theoretical extremes."

She thought for a minute, then said, "Can you imagine where that could lead? The freedom of speech would guarantee your right to recite the Ku Klux Klan Manifesto at a black civil rights meeting. Freedom of religion could allow a Hari Krishna celebration in front of the Mormon Tabernacle."

"And freedom of assembly would allow the Nazis to have a parade through the Jewish community in Skokie."

"So it would. Far be it for me to knock the Constitution, but it seems to me that common sense should play some kind of a role in the whole scheme of things."

"You'd think so, but don't bet on it."

"Can you imagine trying to get on a plane carrying a loaded shotgun because the Constitution gives us the right to bear arms?"

"Two points for common sense!"

"Well, maybe there's hope for us yet."

"Tell that to the ACLU."

She grinned mischievously. "Can you imagine what the ACLU would say about our activities?"

"Probably something like: 'Fie upon you, you perpetrators of malicious malfeasance!'"

She laughed a low, throaty laugh. Wagner smiled at her, thoroughly enjoying her company.

"Are you getting hungry," he asked.

"No," she replied. "You haven't kissed me yet."

"Anything to oblige," he said.

She broke off the kiss abruptly and said, "Now I'm hungry."

"I didn't know I had that effect on you."

"Now you know."

"What kind of pizza do you want tonight?"

"How about Chinese? What's on a Chinese pizza?"

He thought for a minute. "Instead of cheese, you get rice and bean sprouts. The options include bamboo shoots, chow mein noodles, pressed duck, and miniature bird nests. You pour soy sauce over the whole thing. And in the middle there's a slip of paper with your fortune on it."

"You have to keep it out of the soy sauce, of course."

"Of course," he agreed.

"Sounds terrific! Let's go!"

"Wait! You missed the best part. By serving Chinese food as egg roll pizzas, you don't have to use chop sticks. You can eat it with your fingers."

"I think you're getting carried away with all this."

"Maybe you're right. Are you ready?"

"If you make me wait much longer, we'll have to order breakfast."

"Did I ever tell you about my breakfast pizza with scrambled eggs and corn flakes?"

"Please spare me! You'll ruin my appetite."

"If you insist," said Wagner as they left the apartment.

12

The following Monday Wagner got up early to begin his new role as a fisherman. He was somewhat distressed to find that it was raining lightly and the wind was blowing from the north. It would not be a pleasant day on Lake Michigan. Knowing that he would get soaked no matter what he wore, he put on as many wool garments as he could find. He knew that wool stinks when it gets wet, but it still holds in body heat.

He reached Calumet Harbor right at seven. Fletcher was already there looking out on the lake. The sky was gray, the lake was gray, and the waves were about two feet high. It was hardly what they had hoped for. Unfortunately, it wasn't quite bad enough to prohibit them from going out.

"Did you catch the weather forecast?" Wagner asked.

"Yeah. It's supposed to calm down a little."

"Maybe we can stay inside the breakwater for a while to get used to it. Then after it calms down and warms up, we can venture out a little farther."

Two men were there with the boat on a trailer. They were to help launch the boat, then pick it up later that afternoon. They backed the trailer down into the water, released the boat, and secured it to the pier. The choppy waves caused the Starcraft to bump against the rubber padding. Then one of the men came over to Wagner and Fletcher.

"There's a slight change of plans," he said. "We were able to rent a space at the marina just south of Jackson Park. Give us your car keys and we'll take your cars there. That way you won't have to keep loading and unloading the boat. It's also close to the dock where Koster's boats tie up."

That was good news for Wagner. Jackson Park was within reasonable walking distance of his apartment.

"You anchor at marker number 64," the man continued. "Someone from the marina will pick you up and bring you to the dock. If the weather gets worse and you have to come back here, give us a call on the radio and we'll meet you."

Wagner and Fletcher felt rather lonely as they turned and faced the turbulent lake, but Fletcher got behind the steering wheel and started the 55-hp engine. It kicked right over, and they headed out onto the lake. The two men on shore waited until they were underway, then started to move one of the cars to the marina. They would have to come back for the other one.

Visibility was limited by haze on the water, but they were able to see the markers on the breakwater to the northeast. On the shore to the north they could just make out a huge steel mill. To the south lay a series of industrial plants and oil refineries, most of them in neighboring Indiana.

Wagner commented, "I used to fish a lot when I was a kid. The lakes never looked like this, though."

"Mismanagement ruined this lake once," Fletcher replied. "It was nearly dead. Then they started taking care of it better, and now it's coming back."

Wagner looked out and saw a large number of small dead fish floating on the surface.

"It doesn't look very healthy to me," he said. "Look at all those dead fish."

"Those are alewives. They swim up the St. Lawrence Seaway from the Atlantic Ocean. That started when they dug out the seaway to make room for ocean-going vessels. The alewives came in and died by the millions in the fresh water. Then someone got the idea of planting salmon in here to eat the alewives, which were just stinking up the beaches. The salmon gorge themselves, grow like crazy, and now we have some of the best salmon fishing around."

"I'll believe that when I see it. I'm not used to fishing in the shadow of a steel mill."

"OK, put one of those red lures on. We're far enough out to start fishing," said Fletcher as he cut the big motor and started the 6-hp Johnson trolling motor.

Wagner selected a large red Rappala lure, secured it to his line, dropped it over the side, and let out about fifty yards of line. Then he took the wheel while Fletcher did the same with a blue lure. About fifteen minutes later Wagner got a bite, but he missed it. A few minutes later Fletcher had a strike and reeled in a Coho salmon about sixteen inches long. It was not badly hooked, so he threw it back. "They get bigger than this," he said.

They trolled in an elliptical pattern inside the breakwater for about two hours. Fletcher caught two more Coho salmon, and Wagner caught one. Then their lines got tangled together, and they spent half an hour trying to separate them before cutting the remaining mess.

By then it was ten o'clock. The lake was no longer so rough, and the temperature had risen a few degrees.

"I suppose we should move out of the breakwater area and head north," said Fletcher. "We can troll our way up."

"Aye, aye, sir!" said Wagner, who was taking his turn at the wheel. As he headed for the end of the protected area, Fletcher made a communications check with headquarters and the other boat. He succeeded in reaching headquarters, but was still unable to reach Newman and Day, who should have launched from a point ten miles north of them at about ten. They were supposed to stay on the lake until nearly dark.

As the two partners left the shelter of the breakwater, the lake became considerably rougher. After about twenty minutes of being buffeted by the waves, both of them were quite nauseated.

"Did you bring any Dramamine tablets?" asked Fletcher.

"No such luck."

"Well, I needed to lose a few pounds anyway."

"Think positive. Sometimes you can talk yourself out of being seasick."

"I'll try. But don't you go waving a fish under my nose."

The lake gradually calmed, and their nausea stabilized at a level short of actual illness. Neither of them made an attempt to eat lunch, though, let alone drink a beer. They concentrated on their fishing and caught their limit by three o'clock. Wagner got lucky and hooked a seven-pound steelhead trout. That caused both of them to forget their discomfort, at least for a few minutes.

As the lake calmed during the afternoon, more boats joined them. The two men took turns looking through their binoculars at the larger boats, of which there were more than a few. They never did spot either of the Koster cabin cruisers. Fletcher made contact with Newman and Day early in the afternoon and maintained it hourly for the rest of their tour of duty, but the other police team was equally unsuccessful.

At three-thirty they headed for the marina. "I guess we can chalk this one up to practice," said Fletcher.

As they entered the marina, they spotted one of the Koster cruisers. Apparently it had remained there all day. It occurred to them that their job would be a lot simpler if they knew for sure that one of the cruisers would be used to receive the shipment. It was possible, though, that the boats could be there just to draw attention away from a different boat entirely. They found their slip and dropped anchor. Within minutes a man in a small dispatch boat came to pick them up. They took their fish with them, but left their lunch and their beer on the boat. They soon found out that sea sickness doesn't end with arrival back on land. Neither of them was inclined to think much about supper. They just located their respective vehicles and drove home.

The next day was a little easier. Either the lake was less turbulent or their stomachs were becoming accustomed to the motion. They caught more fish. One of the Koster boats went out during the afternoon, but the men aboard just appeared to be fishing, although Wagner didn't see them catch anything. The day passed quickly, and the two partners were surprised to notice how soon four o'clock came.

The third day was stormy. Small boat warnings were announced. Wagner spent most of the day at headquarters catching up on reading an accumulation of papers. On the way home, he drove near the lake. Huge waves were crashing against the shore. Nobody would be going out on a day like that, he thought, unless it would be an ocean-going vessel or an ore ship. As he watched the tempestuous display of nature, it occurred to him that he had only seen two bodies of water which were more subject to storm: Lake Superior and the North Atlantic. But Lake Michigan was rough enough. He had often seen Lake Shore Drive closed because the waves from the lake were lapping across the highway. Just then he was happy to be going to a warm apartment rather than have to battle the lake.

The storm beat itself out that night. By morning it was sunny and calm. Wagner met Fletcher at the marina at seven, and the two spent a beautiful day on the water. They caught their limit of salmon and threw back several more. Both Koster boats came out for a short time, but returned to port without coming near any other boats. Wagner and Fletcher were beginning to feel as if they were on a holiday.

The next day was a carbon copy of the preceding one. The two partners set out with more thoughts about fishing than police work. But as he was trolling, Wagner started to mull over the situation in his mind.

"Hey, Fletch," he said. "I've got an idea."

"What's that?" replied his partner.

"Suppose you were trying to move something from Milwaukee to Chicago on the lake, and you didn't want anyone to know about it. What would be your optimum situation?"

Fletcher thought for a minute. "It would be best at night, but it would be hard to make contact."

"OK, then what?"

"I suppose it would be best when there are lots of boats out here so nobody would pay any attention."

"Right. So you make several tentative moves without doing anything just to create extraneous motion, then schedule your pick-up for a nice Saturday or Sunday, when the lake looks like Dunkirk."

"This weekend?"

"Why not?"

"Well, there's one way to find out."

The next day was Saturday, and the partners went fishing again. It was slightly cooler than the previous two days, but still a nice day. The local fishermen turned out in great numbers.

"One of us will have to watch the traffic while the other one watches the lines," said Wagner.

"Right. This is worse than the Eisenhower Expressway during rush hour."

They moved farther than usual from shore to get away from the smaller boats. Soon the Chicago skyline unfolded in a panorama before them. The sunlight was reflecting from the huge downtown buildings. Wagner shook his head. "After having fished in Wyoming and Canada, I still think this is a helluva funny spot to do any serious fishing."

"Did you catch any Coho salmon there?" asked Fletcher.

"No. Lots of trout and pike. No salmon."

"Well, then, don't knock it."

"I won't. For six weeks of the year, this is the hottest spot in the state. Although that isn't saying a whole lot, considering the alternatives in Illinois."

Just then Fletcher's rod bent over in its holder. He grabbed it and set the hook.

"Cut the engine!" he yelled excitedly. "I've got a good one!"

It soon became apparent that Fletcher had one of those fish on his line that ardent fishermen dream about. The fish slipped his drag until it tired a little, then Fletcher reeled in the lost line. There was no rushing this one. It was big. The minutes passed unnoticed as the strong man fought the equally strong fish, each gaining then losing line. Wagner watched, totally oblivious to where their boat was drifting. He held the landing net eagerly, long before the fish was near the boat.

Fletcher let out a whoop of sheer delight. "Damn!" he said. "This has to be the second-greatest feeling in the world!"

Wagner grinned and strained to get a glimpse of the fish. Finally it came into view, a big silver shape that looked like a torpedo. Fletcher reeled it closer to the boat, and Wagner netted it on the first try. The handle of the landing net bent as he hoisted the big fish into the boat. It was a lunker of a king salmon.

"How much do you think it weighs?" asked Fletcher.

"I don't know. Maybe twenty or thirty pounds."

Fletcher removed the lure carefully and lifted the fish. "It's too bad we don't have a camera," he said.

"We can pick one up one when we get back in," said Wagner.

Fletcher looked thoughtful for a minute. "Nope," he said, and he dropped the fish back into the lake.

Wagner was too stunned to say anything.

"Somebody else should have the thrill of catching him," Fletcher said simply. "Besides, the smaller ones always taste better."

They found that they had drifted quite far south while Fletcher was fighting the fish, so they headed north at a fast trolling speed. They caught three more fish that morning, but it seemed rather anti-climactic after the big one.

When they reached a position close to the marina, they started to check out the other boats through the binoculars. Boats came and went, but they didn't spot either of the Koster cabin cruisers until about three in the afternoon, when they saw one heading northeast. The two reeled in their lines and followed at a distance. The cruiser went out about three miles, far enough to get away from most of the fishing traffic. Wagner kept it in sight while Fletcher drove.

"I see four men. They have fishing rods, but nobody seems to be getting ready to use them."

The cruiser slowed down. Fletcher cut his speed, and the two started trolling again. They just let out about twenty yards of line in case they should have to move quickly.

After a while another large boat came into view from the north. It headed straight for the cabin cruiser.

"Keep your eyes open," said Fletcher. "This may be it."

The other boat pulled up next to the cabin cruiser, and the men on the latter caught a line and pulled the boats together. Wagner saw some cargo being transferred. Then the two boats parted. The entire transaction had taken just minutes. After that, the cabin cruiser headed back toward the marina.

"That's it!" shouted Fletcher. "Call headquarters!"

Wagner got on the radio as Fletcher started back toward the marina. They couldn't hope to keep pace with the larger boat, but they didn't need to.

"Argus six, this is Argus four. Over."

No response.

"Argus six, this is Argus four, come in Argus six. Over"

Nothing.

"Wonderful!" said Fletcher. "Try the Coast Guard."

Wagner looked at the radio card quickly and changed the frequency of the set.

"Sequin Blue, this is Sequin Orange. Over."

No response. Two more attempts. Still no response.

"Damn!" exclaimed Wagner. "This piece of junk works fine until you need it. Then it quits."

"Murphy must have a law about that."

"I'm glad you think it's so funny. We're on our own."

"In that case, we'd better check our hardware."

Wagner opened a panel and removed two plastic bags. He opened them and removed two pistols and some extra clips.

"That boat is headed back to the marina. Why would they go there?"

"They must feel pretty safe. Be sure not to make it obvious that we're following them."

"We're getting close enough to shore that they won't think anything of it. Lots of boats are heading back by now."

The cruiser reached the marina several minutes ahead of them, and they lost sight of it for a while. As they entered the marina, they caught sight of the second Koster boat, but saw no one aboard. Then they saw the boat which they had been following. It was tied to the pier, and the crewmen were still aboard. Fletcher pulled up to the pier, and the two partners got out. They walked nonchalantly toward the boat. All four crewmen were still working. As the two reached the boat, they suddenly drew their guns. Fletcher hollered, "Police! Hold it right there."

Fletcher remained on the pier and covered Wagner as the latter jumped aboard and started to line the four men up. But just then a voice came from inside the cabin.

"Drop your gun and come in here. You on the pier, get over here or your friend is a dead man."

The turn of events happened so suddenly and quietly that no one fifty yards away would have been aware of what was going on there.

Only then did it occur to Wagner that the crews from both boats were on the one cabin cruiser. They had walked into a trap like a couple of rookies.

"Listen to me and do exactly as I say," warned the spokesman for the group. He was a short, middle-aged man wearing a sailor cap and a leather jacket. "One of you go back to your boat with two of my men and take it where they tell you. The rest of us will follow in the cabin cruiser here."

Fletcher had been driving and assumed that he was the one to take the Starcraft. He started toward the smaller boat, and two of the crewmen followed close behind him. Wagner could only imagine one purpose for another excursion on the lake. His mind raced feverishly as he tried to figure a way out of the dilemma.

The two boats began retracing the route which they had just taken. They continued out onto the lake until they had passed all the fishermen and sight-seers. Wagner, guarded by three men, was only too aware of the gravity of the situation. As he looked back toward the Chicago skyline, he noted that it was outlined against a bright blue sky. It didn't seem to him that the world should look so bright on one's last day. It should be all gray and rainy. He thought of Sylvia. She probably would never find out what had happened to him. How could she even ask about him? She still didn't know his name. Maybe the judge would find out for her. Somehow Wagner didn't find that thought very comforting.

About five miles out, Fletcher's boat stopped. This would be it. Wagner considered trying to jump overboard, but realized the futility of such a move. He had been trying to think of something—anything—all the way out, but he was too hopelessly outnumbered. The cabin cruiser pulled up near the Starcraft. Apparently they all wanted to watch.

Suddenly some commotion erupted on the Starcraft. Fletcher pulled out a pistol from somewhere near the steering wheel and dispatched his escorts with two quick shots. Then he opened fire on the cruiser, which was about ten yards away. The crew members on the larger boat were slow to react, but eventually they returned his fire. One of the crewmen was hit in the arm before Fletcher was cut down. With their attention distracted toward the smaller boat, none noticed Wagner for a few moments. As soon as the wounded crewman fell and dropped his gun, Wagner seized the opportunity and made a dive for it. The other crewmen still had their backs to him when he started firing. He shot both of them as well as their wounded companion before they could return a shot in his direction. Then, remembering the man in the cabin, he moved to a position where he could see inside. Cautiously he peered through a window. There he saw the spokesman for the crew cowering behind a chair. Wagner took careful aim and fired. Glass shattered everywhere. It was his last bullet, but it hit the man in the right shoulder.

Wagner quickly picked up another gun and moved cautiously inside the cabin. The man on the floor looked up at him with a terrified expression.

"Don't shoot any more," he pleaded. "I'm Koster. We can work out a deal. This stuff we're carrying is worth millions. There's enough to make us both rich."

Wagner sensed such an overwhelming feeling of disgust that it nauseated him. He shot Koster in the belly without saying a word in reply.

As he went back outside to survey the carnage, the sun was getting lower in the sky. Wagner squinted as he looked out over the water. His only immediate concern was for Fletcher, but the latter was slumped over the driver's seat, his body riddled with bullet holes. None of the others was moving, but he wasn't particularly concerned whether they were dead or alive. He found the ship-to-shore radio and called the Coast Guard. The radio worked fine. He didn't bother to speculate on the difference it might have made if their radio had worked earlier. Instead he simply asked the Coast guard radio operator to relay a message to his headquarters and to send for a launch to be dispatched to his location.

As he waited for the Coast Guard cutter to arrive, Wagner felt a confusion of strong emotions. He was relieved to have escaped with his life, furious at the men who had killed his partner, grieved by the loss of a friend, and surprised at the potential for violence within himself. He could have started to prepare for the trip back, but he didn't feel like it. Let the Coast Guard do it, he thought. He went back inside the cabin and looked around. The cargo was not hard to find. It consisted of a substantial amount of heroin. He thought of tasting it to check the concentration, but he didn't feel like doing that either. He found some beer in a cooler, opened one, and sat down to wait for the Coast Guard.

It was dark back by the time he got back to the marina. Lieutenant Gerhardt was there waiting for him. The police had already impounded the other cabin cruiser. Several of them were busy looking it over.

"You all right, Wagner?" Gerhardt asked.

Wagner nodded without saying anything.

"I'm sorry as hell about Fletcher. He was as good as they come. The chief has gone out to notify his wife."

Wagner nodded a vague acknowledgement and mumbled something unintelligible.

"You sure you're all right?"

"I've been better."

"Can you talk about it?" asked Gerhardt. "We're already

getting inquiries. The commissioner. The mayor's office. The media."

"Tell 'em all to go to hell," said Wagner.

Gerhardt looked almost intimidated. "I can understand. You go home and rest. You can file your report Monday. We'll talk about it then."

Wagner grunted, picked up his gear, and started home.

13

Wagner unlocked the door to his apartment and went in. He dropped his tackle box by the door, then went into the kitchen and dumped the contents of a plastic garbage bag into the sink. It consisted of five cans of beer and six fish. A voice from the distant past demanded that he clean the fish no matter how little he felt like it. He rinsed off the cans of beer and put them in the refrigerator, then prepared to tackle the fish-cleaning chore. Just then the telephone rang. He was sorely tempted to let it ring, but finally decided to answer it. If it was a reporter or Mrs. Fletcher, he would say that they had a wrong number and hang up.

"Hello," he said dully.

"Richard? I've been calling for hours."

"I had to log some overtime today."

"You sound awful. What's wrong?"

"Fletcher got killed this afternoon."

There was no immediate response. She had never met Fletcher, but she knew that he was a good friend. "I'm so sorry," she said. "Are you all right?"

"Physically, yes. Otherwise, I feel like the whole world needs an enema, and I'd like to insert the hose."

It was her turn to be at a loss for words. Finally she said, "If you'd rather be alone, I'll understand, but if you need a shoulder to lean on, I'll come over."

"I'll warn you, I'm in a rotten mood."

"It sounds as if you've earned the privilege. I'll be right over."

Wagner cleaned the fish and took a quick shower. He had just finished drying off when Sylvia arrived. He was still unshaven and uncombed. That plus his sunburnt face gave him a strangely wild appearance, but she resisted the impulse to mention it. He finished shaving and combed his hair while she watched from the doorway.

"Have you eaten yet?" she asked.

"No. I didn't think I was hungry, but all of a sudden I'm starved. I'll fry one of those fish if you'll help me eat it."

"Why don't you sit down and relax while I do the cooking," she said.

Wagner complied. He expected her to ask about the incident on the lake, but she didn't. She seemed to be waiting for him to get around to it in his own good time. Finally he took a deep breath and started to relate the incident. He didn't leave anything out. When he told about Fletcher's death, he added, "He had that extra gun stashed there all the time. He could have shot those two goons and made a break for it. Instead he waited until the cruiser was in range. He gave me the chance I needed by exposing himself to certain death. What can you say about a guy like that?"

Wagner was as close to tears as he had ever been in his adult life.

"I'd say he must have thought as much of you as you did of him," she replied. Then she came to him, sat on his lap, and said, "I'm very grateful to him, even though I never met him."

For the first time that evening, Wagner smiled. "I guess the one consolation after losing a good partner is the knowledge that he wasn't my only partner."

Then they just sat together for a time without talking.

After a while, Sylvia made a salad to go with the fish, and they ate a late supper. She had eaten earlier, and his appetite was affected by the trauma of the day's events, so neither of them was able to eat much. They cleared the table and went into the living room. Wagner picked out a record and put it on the stereo. It was piano music, Mendelssohn's "Song Without Words." Then he joined her on the couch.

"The next few days will be a nightmare," he said. "There will be a round of interrogations from every level of law enforcement. Then there will be a funeral to attend. Somewhere along the line I'll have to explain to Fletcher's shrew of a wife how I got her husband killed. There will be people from the media…"

She put her finger against his lips. "All of that can wait until Monday. Right now you belong to me, and you don't have to talk about any of it."

"Usually it depresses me to talk about my work, and I assume that it would depress anyone else. But now for some reason I need to talk about it. I don't want to be left alone with my thoughts for a change."

"I'll stay with you for as long as you want me to."

"I have to tell you something. I probably won't be able to tell this to anyone else. I could have brought Koster in alive, but I didn't. I gut-shot him and let him bleed to death. It didn't even occur to me to try to save his life."

She thought about that for a minute without changing expression, then said, "Well, while you're at it, you might as well feel guilty for shooting those others in the back instead of waiting for them to turn around. I'll bet Roy Rogers would have done that. Then they'd have shot you instead of the other way around."

"Yes, but Koster was wounded and helpless."

"As long as he was alive, he was neither. He still had all the power he could buy. You might as well feel sorry for stepping on a cockroach."

"You seem to know quite a lot about him."

"He was one of the people I'd been researching. Just off

the record, you saved our organization some time and effort. Our mutual friend seems particularly hostile toward people who bring in large quantities of narcotics."

Wagner smiled humorlessly. "Maybe I'll get a bonus."

"Right now I'm just glad that you're still in one piece."

"Oh, I'd have been in one piece. It's just that it would have been soaking up Lake Michigan by now."

She shuddered involuntarily. "Don't talk like that."

"No, I shouldn't. Tonight when I try to sleep, all of this will probably catch up with me. Right now it seems vague and unreal, as if I'd dreamt the whole thing. It will probably hit me like a ton of bricks when I go to the office and find someone else sitting in Fletcher's chair."

"How long did you work together?"

"Three years. We were in a lot of scrapes together, but nothing like this one. Damn! It just doesn't seem possible. This morning he caught a big fish and looked like the happiest guy in the world. I'll never forget how he looked fighting that salmon and yelling, 'This must be the second-greatest feeling in the world.' Now he's lying on a slab with his chest full of holes. All in the same day."

She leaned her head against him. "Try not to dwell on it. Concentrate on the good memories."

He sighed. "I'm really glad you're here. I thought I wanted to be alone, but that would have been morbid."

"I'm glad I was able to help."

"You're some lady. It's incredible that I still don't even know your name."

"Is it important?"

"Not especially, although it occurred to me this afternoon that if something happened to one of us, the other one wouldn't even know whom to ask about. We'd have to trace each other's phone number or check with the apartment manager."

"If you really want to know my name, I'll tell you," she said as she kissed him on the neck.

"If you keep doing that, I probably couldn't remember it anyway."

She kissed him again. "I'm the best friend you've got in the world. And I'm more relieved than I can tell you that you came through that mess today. I can't imagine a world without you in it. Just hold me tight for a while."

He held her close to him, and neither of them spoke for a few minutes. Then Wagner said, "I don't want you to leave."

"Then I won't."

The next Monday Wagner went to police headquarters with considerable apprehension. He could imagine several possible scenarios for the day, and none of them was pleasant. However, he was unprepared for the one which actually occurred. Lieutenant Gerhardt called him into his office and closed the door.

"Sit down, Wagner," he said. He looked uncomfortable. "I'll need your report on the shooting as soon as you can get it ready. Then you're to be suspended again. This time with pay, though."

Wagner was too surprised to say anything.

"Here's what happened," the lieutenant continued. "It seems that Koster was just a relatively small cog in a larger machine. That machine was very unhappy about losing the shipment that was on the boat Saturday. So over the weekend they got their lawyers to figure out how to make a big stink about it."

Gerhardt looked very much out of character. He obviously didn't like what he was being forced to do.

"What it all boils down to is that you were outside the city limits when you did your John Wayne act. We had no jurisdiction out there. Now someone's trying to charge you with criminal assault and manslaughter."

Wagner started to stammer something, but Gerhardt held up his hand.

"Don't get excited. You have the backing of the whole department. There's no way they can pull this off. I'm sure they know that. But we have to suspend you until we get a ruling on it. Just write your report, then take a little vacation. Stay in the area and call in every morning. We'll get this whole mess straightened out, and you can pick up where you left off."

Wagner was still too dumbfounded to speak.

Gerhardt, obviously embarrassed, added, "Don't let this get you down, Wagner. Personally, I think this business stinks, but I don't have enough clout to do anything but wait."

"So I'm supposed to go and twiddle my thumbs while I wait to find out if I'm to be tried for defending myself."

Gerhardt winced at that remark. "It won't go that far."

"Is there anything else?"

"Just one thing. Mrs. Fletcher would like to talk to you. The memorial service is tomorrow afternoon. She'd like to see you today."

"Couldn't she call me herself?"

"She couldn't remember your first name, and there are a lot of Wagners in the phone book."

"OK. I'll go and see her after I finish the report. I'll be at the funeral tomorrow. I doubt if I'll be asked to serve as a pallbearer, though."

"She had his body cremated."

Wagner thought, "She probably wants to keep his ashes in an urn on the mantle so she can nag at him the way she always has." His expression betrayed his negative sentiment.

"At first I was surprised that she didn't know your first

name, but now it makes more sense," said Gerhardt, picking up on Wagner's sour mood.

Wagner shrugged. "I'm glad something makes sense to you, Lieutenant. I haven't had that feeling for some time."

Gerhardt was at a loss for words and felt relieved when Wagner left.

Wagner finished his written report before noon and got a light lunch at the cafeteria. He was looking forward to his visit with Mrs. Fletcher about as much as a trip to the dentist with an impacted wisdom tooth. He drove slowly to the Fletcher home about half an hour west of his, realizing that he hadn't been there in the last two years. He parked in front of the modest white house and braced himself for the ordeal.

A neighbor lady answered the door. Mrs. Fletcher was in the living room with another woman. Nobody offered to introduce the other two women. Mrs. Fletcher looked up as Wagner entered the room. Her narrow face and pointed nose had not changed, nor did her features look any softer in her grief. Wagner couldn't tell whether she had been crying or not.

"Thank you for coming," she said. "Please sit down."

Wagner complied.

"I understand that you were with him when it happened."

"That's right."

"Please tell me about it."

Wagner took a deep breath and began to relate the details of the previous Saturday. In his usual laconic way, he boiled it down to the bare essentials. He neglected to mention the part about his encounter with Koster, but emphasized the fact that Fletcher had sacrificed his own life in order to save Wagner's. He left no doubt that he regarded Fletcher as an exceptionally brave and unselfish man.

After he had completed his narrative, he paused expectantly for her to ask questions. She relieved his anxiety somewhat by not asking any. She simply nodded as if to indicate her approval.

"Thank you for coming here," she said. "I realize that it wasn't a very pleasant task for you."

Wagner could hardly argue with that remark, so he said nothing.

"I know that my husband regarded you highly. I think he just proved how highly. May I ask a favor on his behalf?"

"Of course," Wagner replied apprehensively.

"Tomorrow at the memorial service, would you sit with the family?"

"I'd consider it an honor."

"Thank you. We'll see you then." She extended her hand to him, and he grasped it in a brief handshake.

Wagner departed with confused thoughts about this unloved and unlovely woman. He had never liked her, and she had never shown him anything but resentment, but at least on this one occasion she had conducted herself with genuine dignity. He felt a little ashamed for the thoughts he had had about her. He had arrived with a feeling of dread and left with a sense of peace toward her.

14

The next morning Wagner was awakened from a sound sleep by the ringing of the telephone. He picked up the receiver and responded before noticing that it was only six-thirty.

"Good morning, Mr. Wagner," said a strange voice. "This is Benjamin."

"I didn't know you were still talking to me."

"We've been contacting you through your associate for reasons of security, but I have some information for you which is better transmitted directly."

"Let me find a pencil," said Wagner. "OK, go ahead."

"First, let me offer my condolences. I understand that you and your partner were quite close."

"Thank you. Yes, we were." Wagner rubbed his eyes to clear them.

"We are also aware of the legal action being taken against you by a certain organization."

"You don't miss much, do you?"

"We try not to. By the way, don't bother looking in the newspaper for an account of your escapade. You won't find one."

"Did the city suppress it?"

"No, the syndicate did. I doubt if the city could have. Freedom of the press and all that sort of thing, you know."

"It sounds like we're dealing with some real hard-ball players this time."

"That we are. You ruffled some feathers Saturday. Not by

eliminating Koster and his associates. They weren't exactly small fry, but maybe medium-sized. By intercepting that cargo, you fouled up an operation worth several million dollars that took nearly a month to set up."

"Are they out to get me?"

"Yes, but they'd prefer to use our own legal system to do it. They have their own legal branch working on the assault charge. They also know how Koster died."

Wagner caught his breath as the implications of that bit of information registered.

"There aren't many secrets left, are there?"

"Apparently not. But we'd like to make use of your suspension to upset their plans a bit."

"I'm listening."

"Every lawyer finds himself in the position of defending someone whom he'd just as soon see convicted. That's part of our system. But there are some lawyers who specialize in protecting hard-core criminals and their organizations. That's what we're dealing with now."

"That's what I figured."

"The lawyer who filed the assault charges against you is named Marshall. Do you know him?"

"No, but that's a dandy name for an aspiring lawyer."

"I doubt if this one has any relatives on the Supreme Court, past or present. He heads a law firm which takes on just enough legitimate cases to lend a veneer of respectability. Their main activity is to protect the interests of some major-league syndicate figures."

"So what can we do about it?"

"That's what I want you to help us decide. Mr. Marshall has a home in Oak Park and an apartment in Chicago. I thought you might like to look them over and make a recommendation as to some appropriate action we might take against him."

"All right, but it would be helpful if someone could check

into his property insurance to see what is covered. If we're going in for some high-class vandalism, we don't want to run afoul the insurance companies."

"That should be relatively simple to find out. I'll get back to you in a couple of days. Here are the two addresses. You won't find either listed in the telephone directory."

Wagner copied down the two addresses, one in the most exclusive part of Oak Park, the other in a high-rise apartment building on North Michigan Avenue, just off Lake Michigan. Not many people could have afforded either of the two homes.

Since the funeral service was not until afternoon, Wagner decided to check out the apartment that morning. It was on the fourteenth floor of the high-rise. Marshall apparently maintained it just for the convenience of having a place closer to his downtown office. However, a second possibility occurred to Wagner. By bribing the doorman, he learned that an attractive young woman was living in Marshall's apartment. Wagner wondered if he was being tested. Was he expected to recommend that they try to blackmail Marshall for keeping a mistress? Wagner thought he could do better than that. Blackmail wasn't exactly his style. Somehow he couldn't imagine that it was Judge Carrol's style either. He would have to check out the home in Oak Park to see if there might be a better opportunity there.

He returned to his apartment in time to eat lunch and change clothes for the funeral. Actually it was just a memorial service in a small Methodist church near the Fletcher home. Since his body had been cremated after the required coroner's examination, there was no actual funeral or interment. The autopsy was simply standard procedure for deaths resulting from gunshot wounds.

The service was mercifully short. There was no eulogy, just a short summation of the main events in Fletcher's thirty-seven-year life. There were few flowers. There was organ music, but no singing. The minister gave a short message on the transitory nature of life and recited from the Book of Job: "Man born of woman is of few days and full of trouble. He springs up like a flower and withers away; like a fleeting shadow, he does not endure." Then he read a passage from the New Testament which expressed the confident hope that the deceased had gone on to a better life. There were a few tears, but no sobbing or wailing. All in all, it was a service marked by somber dignity. The family section consisted of Mrs. Fletcher, an older brother of the deceased and his wife from Kansas, and a younger sister who taught grade school in Wisconsin. With Wagner added, they almost filled one row. The other guests consisted of about twenty church members and the usual show of support from uniformed police officers from all over the area. Wagner only recognized a few and doubted if more than a dozen had known Fletcher. It was not a very impressive representation, but Fletcher had not been the kind of man who made many close friends.

As the service ended and the participants filed out, Wagner noticed Lieutenant Gerhardt among the other police officers. The lieutenant looked back at him, but then avoided him and left without speaking to him. The Fletchers invited Wagner to join them for a meal hosted by the church, but he politely declined, saying that he had other plans. Actually he felt that the formalities between Mrs. Fletcher and himself had been stretched to the limit, and he preferred to leave it at that.

He didn't feel like going back to his apartment, so he drove to Oak Park in the western suburbs and located the Marshall home. It was an elegant brick house on a large lot. It had several oak trees in the front yard and a swimming pool in the back. Wagner made a mental note to remember to bring his binoculars the next day in order to get a better view of certain details. It appeared that Marshall had a family. Wagner would have to be careful to make sure that no harm came to them.

The next day Wagner returned with binoculars, paper for sketching, and a clip board. He was dressed in an approximation of the uniform worn by electrical company employees. At one point he walked through the neighbors' yards with the clip board and read the meters. Then he moved to several different positions and looked through the binoculars. The large space between houses allowed him to do this without too much concern about being observed. After about two hours, he had a fairly detailed sketch of the layout of the house and the yard. Then he went home and studied the sketch for a long time while he drank beer and listened to Chopin.

By the time Benjamin called again, Wagner had a detailed plan ready. Benjamin had the insurance information that Wagner had requested, and they started coordinating details. It took several more calls for them to complete the arrangements, but within two days they were ready. Wagner asked to have Sylvia go along as a driver, mainly because she had gotten so caught up in the adventure of the scheme that she didn't want to miss it.

The next Thursday night the weather forecast called for an eighty percent chance of thunderstorms. They decided that the time was ripe to put the plan into operation. They would need rain as part of the plan. Sylvia called her contact to initiate the action.

At two-thirty in the morning two vehicles approached the Marshall home. The larger vehicle was a medium-sized tank truck. The other was a rented car, which Sylvia drove. She parked across the street from the house, having turned off the lights a block away. Wagner got out and conferred briefly with the two men in the truck. The weather was ideal for their purposes. Wagner removed some sections of guttering material from the truck and carried them to the house. One of the men from the truck grabbed the end of a long hose, such as those used by trucks carrying heating oil, and started toward the swimming pool. The other man walked to one of the oak trees in the front yard and began working on it. The rain was coming down steadily, accented by an occasional flash of lightning and a clap of thunder.

Wagner moved to the down spout on one corner of the house. He removed the section which carried the rain water away from the house and substituted three sections from the truck. Then he took out a glass cutter, knelt by a basement window, and cut a hole in it. With a piece of plastic tubing he completed the new conduit, and the rain water from the roof started gushing into the basement of the house.

By that time, the man who had been working on the tree was finished. He picked up his equipment and climbed back into the cab of the truck. A few minutes later, the man with the hose had also finished his job. He reeled in the long hose, got back into the truck, and drove away.

About five minutes later there was an explosion which sounded very much like thunder, and the big oak tree fell across the garage of the house.

"He knew his business," remarked Wagner admiringly. "He dropped that oak right on target."

Then Sylvia put the idling car in gear and the two drove away.

They had to wait until the next afternoon for a newspaper account of their mischief, but the radio and television news picked it up much sooner: "Oak Park police are investigating a highly unusual case of vandalism. The act occurred at the home of Henry G. Marshall, a prominent local attorney. Someone detonated an explosive charge against an oak tree in the front yard, causing it to fall across the two-car garage. In the garage were a Porsche sports car and a Cadillac sedan, both of which were badly damaged.

"At the same time, someone channeled the rain water from the roof into the basement of the house by cutting a hole in the window and re-arranging the guttering. The addition of several precisely cut sections indicates that the act was carefully planned and executed.

"The final act of vandalism is virtually without precedent. The vandals somehow managed to pour a large amount of liquefied pig manure into the swimming pool. The amount is estimated at between one hundred and two hundred gallons. The stench is incredible, and with warm weather approaching, it is likely to constitute a health hazard. Public officials have ordered the pool covered until someone figures out how to get rid of the offensive substance.

"An unidentified informant has offered some insight into the probable cause of the bizarre incident. He stated, and I quote, 'The odor is an indication of what some people think of lawyers who make a practice of defending mobsters,' end of quote."

Wagner sat back and smiled. Then he picked up the phone and dialed a number.

"Lieutenant Gerhardt, please," he said.

A minute later came the reply. "Gerhardt speaking."

"This is Wagner checking in. Any word on the charges?"

"Nothing new, Wagner. You can just continue taking life easy."

"I'll do that."

The evening newspaper showed a picture of the Marshall garage with the oak tree leaning across it. The story was essentially the same as that carried by the radio and TV news broadcasts, but added an update:

"A spokesman for the insurance company carrying

Marshall's home-owners' policy indicated that the home was not covered for vandalism. If the flooding or the fallen tree had been the result of the storm, the policy would have covered the costs of repair and replacement. But since the damage was deliberate, the Marshall policy will not cover any of the costs, which are estimated at between $75,000 and $100,000.

"Investigators for the Oak Park Police Department are puzzled by the incident. None of them had ever seen such a carefully planned and executed act of wanton destruction."

Sylvia came to his apartment as soon as she got off work. She prepared one of the salmon for baking, then read the newspaper account of the incident.

"Have you thought of the possible consequences of this?" she asked.

"You mean what could happen to me?"

"No. I was thinking about what could happen to Marshall. The fact that he has been identified publicly as an associate of the syndicate reduces his value to them. It also ruins his credentials for legitimate practice. Our evening's entertainment in the rain could prove to be very costly to poor Mr. Marshall in more ways than one."

"Well, I'd say offhand that it has worked out better than we'd expected, thanks to the extensive media coverage. So much of what we've done has never been reported. Look at all the time we spent in the shoe business. We never saw a line about it in the papers. But actually we didn't want any publicity. We were just doing an elimination act, and the less said about it, the better. This is different. If we can ruin a major figure in the syndicate without laying a hand on anybody, we're ahead of the game."

"By the way, I heard from my contact today," she said. "He called me at work, which is unusual, but he just wanted me to pass on to you how delighted he was with our latest caper."

"I'm glad that you're glad that he's glad."

"But aren't you glad that he's glad?"

"I'd be gladder if I could quit thinking about Marshall's wife and kids. They must be in a real quandary about all this."

She smiled. "I hope you never lose that quality. We're engaged in a rather rotten business, but we do it only because the conventional way is ineffectual. I just hope we never lose sight of that fact."

"You're still the idealist, aren't you?"

"So are you," she replied. "Sometimes you try to hide it behind a macho façade, but it's still there."

"God help us if we ever start doing these kinds of things because it amuses us!"

"I think I have you figured out," she said. "You thought it would be hilarious to pump Marshall's swimming pool full of pig crap. After you'd done it, you gloated about it for a little while, but then you got to thinking about the two kids who were looking forward to using that pool, and it spoiled your fun."

"Touché, D'Artagnan!"

"And now you won't even bother to deny it."

"Well, let's see now. What do we make of a lady who extols the noblest of virtues, yet cheers for me while I'm out earning notches for my gun? I doubt if you'll get many nominations for the Nobel Peace Prize either."

She crossed her arms and looked at him stubbornly. "All right, Dr. Freud. When you boil it all down, we see eye to eye on nearly all of this. So what are we arguing about?"

"Who's arguing? I'm just humoring you."

"Humoring me? Why you patronizing son of a…"

But by then he had grabbed her and was kissing her. When he finally released her, she had to gasp for breath.

"It's no fair ending an argument that way," she said.

"Would you rather continue?"

For an answer, she put her arms around him and gave him

another long kiss. Then she held him at arms' length, looked into his eyes, grinned, and said, "Wouldn't it have been funny if you'd picked the wrong house."

15

The next morning Wagner found an article in the newspaper which totally dumbfounded him. He was still reading the details when the telephone rang. It was Sylvia.

"Did you see the article on page three of the Tribune?" She asked.

"I just read it. So Vickers is dead."

"I've been researching him for two weeks. Just when I'd concluded that he was beyond our reach, his wife killed him."

"The paper doesn't mention a motive. Do you know why she did it?"

"No idea. I can think of several possibilities, but she hasn't said, and nobody has offered a plausible explanation."

"I'll check with the department. Somebody must know something."

"OK. See you tonight."

Wagner hung up and re-read the article. Vickers, the alleged head of a syndicate empire, was dead at the age of 52, shot once in the temple by his wife of 28 years. She had called the police and admitted the act. Thus, a man who lived behind an iron fence and was guarded by professional watchmen died at the hand of the person who seemed the least likely to want to harm him. Why did she do it? Could there have been another woman? Could she have just found out about his connections to organized crime? It seemed that nobody knew.

Wagner laid the paper down, finished his coffee, and went for his morning run. It was getting warmer, and he was drenched with sweat by the time he finished. It felt good, though, to loosen his leg muscles and test his lungs. It always gave him a feeling of well-being to have his body in good working order. He returned to his apartment and showered to the strains of Beethoven's <u>Third Symphony</u>.

After his shower, Wagner called Lieutenant Gerhardt. The latter had no information about the Vickers case. He had also received no indication that Marshall's embarrassment might make any difference as to the disposition of Wagner's case.

Wagner felt frustrated as he hung up. He was being paid for doing nothing. Summer was coming, and he couldn't make any specific plans. He felt too restless to stay inside, but had no good reason to go anywhere. He was still pondering the alternatives when the phone rang again. It was Sylvia again.

"I just heard from my contact," she said. "Something big is in the works. You're to be in on it."

"I'll have to check with my social secretary and see if I can work it into my schedule."

"Try hard. They want to see you at ten a.m."

"Let's see. I think I'm free then. My appointment with the governor isn't until noon."

"Terrific! I'm so pleased!"

"Who and where?"

"You and I at my place. There will also be two others from the organization, but they don't have names."

"More secrets. OK, I'll be there."

Wagner just had time to straighten up his kitchen, change clothes, and drive to Sylvia's apartment house. She was already there, but the others had not arrived yet, so she was able to greet him somewhat more warmly than she would have otherwise.

"That was nice," he said. "Why don't we just keep quiet and not open the door when the others arrive."

"I will if you will," she teased.

She was still in a light mood when the doorbell rang.

"Shall we answer it?" she asked.

"Let's flip a coin," he replied. Then he went through the motions of flipping a quarter.

"Nuts!" he said. "We have to answer it."

She opened the door and admitted two casually dressed men of about forty. Wagner could not recall ever having seen either of them before. Since everyone knew the general nature of the business, they dispensed with preliminary formalities. Sylvia led them to a table, and they all sat down. She sat on Wagner's right side and deliberately rested her leg against his. He wondered if she would move it to test his ability to act as if nothing were happening, but she sat still.

The shorter of the two men opened a folder and revealed a stack of papers, but he did not offer to share the contents. He was apparently conducting the meeting.

"You are aware, of course, that Vickers is dead," he said.

Wagner and Sylvia nodded affirmatively.

"You are also aware that he controlled a variety of activities all over the country and some even beyond."

"I've heard rumors to that effect," said Wagner. "I don't know how many of them are true."

"We don't need to go into that right now. The significant fact is that there will be a big power struggle from several factions to take his place. It's already started, in fact."

"Anybody we know?" asked Wagner.

"Yes, but the biggest contenders are from Miami and Las Vegas."

Wagner let out a low whistle. Then he said, "Would anyone care to explain to me what we're doing playing in this league? This is federal-level activity. I don't know about you folks, but I'm just a few weeks removed from painting a dope peddler's ass yellow. I mean, isn't this pushing things a bit?"

"We came here to get your opinion on certain matters," replied one of the men. "Of course, the feds are watching these people. They've been watching them for years. But they rarely catch anyone doing anything illegal. Sometime soon there will be a high-level meeting of the principal contenders. It will be a closely guarded secret, but a lot of people will know about it, including the feds. And they won't be able to do anything about it because there's no law against having a meeting."

"Right," said Wagner. "Freedom of assembly it's called. The Constitution guarantees it."

The man looked irritated and tried to ignore the comment. He continued, "So they'll have their meeting under the tightest security they can manage. Of course, the feds will be there as close as they can get with enough electronic equipment to monitor Mars. And we'll be there trying to pull something without getting caught by either of them."

"Just where do I fit into all of this?" asked Wagner.

"The head of our group wants you to help us arrange some appropriate entertainment for the occasion."

"Wonderful. So now I'm on the entertainment committee. I just hope this meeting won't be on Lake Michigan. I didn't do so well on my last assignment as water safety director."

The taller of the two men frowned. "You don't seem to be taking this very seriously," he said.

"Oh, I'm taking it seriously enough. You're talking suicide. I consider that pretty damned serious. Do you realize what kind of security precautions those people will be taking for a meeting like this? It would be like Yalta."

"But where else would you catch so many of their big guns together? And their security will be directed against the conventional law enforcement agencies."

"Don't you believe it," Wagner countered. "They trust each other about as far as I can throw you. Each group will be watching for the others to pull something. They'll really be on their toes."

The shorter of the two men looked annoyed. "We didn't

come here to debate whether or not to act on this tip. We came to ask your advice on how to do it. You don't have to be concerned about taking part in the execution of the plan."

Wagner looked somewhat surprised. "I wouldn't miss it for the world. Let's get to work."

"That's better. Your colleague here has been researching the various organizations. Let's hear from her now."

Sylvia spoke without notes. "There are two Chicago-based organizations which would have something to say about anyone filling Vickers' position. Those are the gangs headed by Leone and Murchison. Leone has narcotics ties with Miami, and Murchison has gambling and prostitution connections with Las Vegas. That's how the syndicate people in those cities get involved in this. The whole apparatus is quite intricate, and we don't have it entirely figured out yet."

"Don't feel bad," Wagner interrupted. "Nobody else does either."

Sylvia continued. "What we have established is that Vickers controlled a variety of enterprises through different organizations, some of them legitimate, most of them not. It seems unlikely that anyone else knew the full extent of his operation. He must have carried it all in his head. He probably didn't dare write anything down."

"And now that he is gone, the largest of his subordinate groups are jockeying for position to control as much of the action as they can reconstruct," said the taller of the two men.

"Right," said Sylvia. "The meeting will most likely be attended by Leone, Murchison, the interested parties from Miami and Las Vegas, and who knows who else."

"One small detail," Wagner interjected. "Do we know where or when this great meeting of the minds is to take place?"

"Not definitely," replied Sylvia, "But we have a pretty good idea. The funeral will give them a pretext for gathering here.

That sets the time, at least in a general sense. The place follows logically. Vickers' estate has a better security system than any other place in the state, with the possible exception of the state penitentiary."

"That makes sense," said Wagner, "But it sure doesn't give us much time."

"If we could have met sooner, we would have," replied the shorter man dourly. Wagner decided that he didn't like the man very much.

"We'll know very soon if we're right," said Sylvia. "The feds are watching all parties concerned, and we're monitoring their communications. In effect, they're doing our surveillance work for us."

"So we have to assume that the meeting will take place in two or three days at the Vickers mansion, and if we're wrong, we go back to the drawing board."

"I don't think we're on the wrong track," Sylvia said. "Everything points in that direction."

Wagner threw up his hands. "Then all you need from me is how to hit the house with the FBI and half the mafia guarding it. Right?"

The shorter man frowned again. "Something like that, but you didn't have to put it in those terms."

"It would help if I knew what resources are available," said Wagner, ignoring the objection.

The taller man replied, "That's hard to answer. I'd say that cost is no object, but time is. Given sufficient time, nearly anything can be bought, but we have only two or three days."

"Fine. What's the weather forecast?"

"The long-range forecast is for some cloudiness, but no rain," replied Sylvia. "Wind and visibility look fine."

"Fine for what? What we need is a blizzard."

"Not too likely in June. Sorry."

"Does anyone have an aerial photograph of the place? A floor plan would also help."

"Aerial photo, yes. Floor plan, no. But we do have a schematic made from descriptions made by a former house maid."

For the next two hours the four of them went over the data that had been gathered. Gradually a plan took shape. The taller of the two men made a list of requirements that staggered Wagner's imagination, but the man never hesitated for a moment.

It was after noon when they finished their work. Sylvia offered to make lunch for all of them, but the two visitors declined, saying that they had to get started with their part of the scheme. Wagner had nothing pressing to do at all, so he accepted her invitation. He watched her as she prepared soup and sandwiches. She looked tense.

"This business has you rattled, doesn't it?" he asked.

"I never had any notion of getting in this deep," she said.

"At least your part in it is just about finished. You did the research work and supplied the necessary intelligence information. Now all you have to do is evaluate the communications between the various federal agencies."

"Your part isn't finished, though. I wish you would stay out of this."

"I need to see it through. I never did like making up a dirty job for somebody else to do. Besides, I'll be anxious to see if we can pull this off."

"I know. You'd love to make a big score against the mob while the feds stand there with their hands in their pockets. But has it occurred to you recently that you could wind up in prison for this? That's assuming the gangsters don't get you first."

"We've both had to face that possibility ever since we got involved in this business," he said. "But do you realize that I could spend thirty years on the police force and never get a chance to do anything significant against organized crime? I can't just sit this one out."

"I know that, and I respect you for it. I just wish it weren't so damned dangerous."

"Oh, maybe we'll get lucky and they'll call the whole thing off."

"Or maybe our friends won't be able to find all the hardware you ordered."

"They'll probably lose the list."

"Or maybe the hoods will decide to hold the meeting in neutral territory."

"Like Disneyland."

"That would be smart," she said. "They could all wear funny masks and blend right in."

"Sure. Why would anyone want to hold a meeting in Chicago?"

"Maybe they hadn't heard that Illinois is being boycotted for meetings because it didn't pass the Equal Rights Amendment."

"I'd completely forgotten about that. Why didn't you bring it up at the meeting?"

"It didn't seem appropriate for me to bring it up, since I was the only woman present. I was hoping you'd think of it.'

"Sorry. It isn't my problem."

"Male chauvinist!"

"Do you realize that chauvinism actually refers to an exaggerated sense of importance attached to one's country or race? It is therefore inappropriately applied to men who realize that a woman's place is in the kitchen or the bedroom."

"Now you're really asking for it. See if I ever cook another meal for you, you sexist boor!"

Wagner sighed deeply. "That hurt," he said. "You really shouldn't call me names. I'm quite sensitive, you know."

"You're about as sensitive as Dick Butkus," she remarked with a grin.

"Better looking, though."

"How long do you plan to keep this up?"

"Until you relent and beg my pardon for hurting my feelings."

"You're impossible," she said as she hugged him.

"Actually, possibility reflects an absolute value where relative terms would be more…"

She curtailed his argument with an enthusiastic kiss.

16

For the next two days there were many indications of frantic activity. Wagner received frequent calls in which information was sometimes requested, sometimes given. The most important message came from Sylvia, and she waited to deliver it in person.

"The meeting has been set. My guess was right. It's for ten o'clock tomorrow night after the funeral at the Vickers estate."

"Bingo! That's a relief. I don't know how we would have adjusted if they'd decided to hold it anywhere else."

"We wouldn't have had time to adjust. I really can't imagine them holding it anywhere else, though. It's hardly the type of conference one holds at the Holiday Inn."

"Did you get that from the FBI?"

"Yes. They've been watching all the principal performers in the show and taping their conversations."

"Do you suppose they've been listening in on us?"

"If they are, they're doing it very well. We don't have any such indication."

"Then let's get on with it."

"I do have one concern," she said.

"What's that?"

"The Vickers had several servants. Is there any danger of innocent bystanders getting caught in this?"

"That occurred to me, too, but it isn't likely. Mrs. Vickers has been arrested for murder. Their children are grown and living out of state. As for the servants, it isn't likely that anyone would be allowed to remain in the house while this meeting is going on unless that individual was in on the operation. So much for innocent bystanders."

"I guess that's the best we can hope for. It seems that there are no absolute guarantees."

"That's right. At best, this is a calculated risk for everyone involved."

"I just hope it's worth it," she said.

"If we can somehow eliminate four kingpins of organized crime, we'll be accomplishing something that the judicial system of the whole country won't match any time soon."

She looked him squarely in the eyes. "Then dammit, let's do it!"

"That's my person!" he said.

"Person? When this party is over, I'm going to take you out to celebrate. Then I'll show you what it's like to have more woman than you can handle."

Several possible responses flashed across Wagner's mind, but he just grinned.

The next evening Wagner drove to a small airport in the western part of DuPage County, just west of the Chicago area. The little-used strip was deserted except for three men, who were working beside a medium-sized helicopter at the far end of the runway. Wagner parked his car in the small lot and walked out to the helicopter. He recognized one of the men as the one who had planted the explosive charge on Marshall's oak tree. The others were obviously the pilot and a mechanic. The demo man looked up as Wagner approached.

"How's it coming?" Wagner asked.

"I've just about got it," the man replied. He was working with a section of pipe about a foot in diameter. "This has to be the biggest shaped charge I've ever made. I usually use the bottom half of a champagne bottle."

"Well, since we couldn't find a 500-pound bomb on such short notice, this will have to do."

"It should work. I got the biggest funnel I could find to form the cone. Then I packed the pipe full of plastic explosive. It's dual primed with electric blasting caps. I checked out all the components this afternoon and double-checked the stand-off distance. It should make one helluva hole."

"Let's just hope the blast goes straight down, like it's supposed to," said the pilot. "I get a little nervous with you popping off a charge that close to the chopper."

"No problem there. That's why they call it a shaped charge."

Wagner then looked at the helicopter. It was a sleek, late model machine, and it looked very expensive.

"That's a pretty fancy chopper," he commented. "Where did they get it?"

The pilot answered, "From a private airfield. It belonged to Mr. Vickers. We didn't think he'd mind if we borrowed it."

Wagner grinned. "You don't say. This gets better all the time."

Two hours later an FBI agent named Dodson was watching the Vickers estate from a grove of trees near the entrance. He was in radio contact with a control van.

"Harper six, this is Harper two, over."

"This is six, over."

"This is two. A convoy of approximately six vehicles has just entered the front gate of the estate. Over."

"This is Harper six. Can you identify any of them? Over."

"This is Harper two. Negative. They are all large sedans,

but it is getting too dark for me to identify them in more detail. Over."

"This is six. Stay where you are and inform me of any new developments. Over."

"This is two. Willco. Out."

Dodson replaced the receiver and picked up his binoculars. He tried to read the license numbers on the cars, but was unable. It hardly mattered, though. He knew that a crew with special infra-red cameras would be taking pictures of everything. Then what would they do with the pictures? They already knew who was attending the meeting and why they were there. What good would all this information do? There was nothing they could do about any of it. Dodson felt a tremendous sense of frustration as he stood there, knowing that a high-level meeting of organized crime was being conducted right under his nose, and he had no authority to intervene in any way. As he looked through the binoculars, he could see guards with German shepherd dogs patrolling the fence.

Soon it was completely dark. There were a few lights inside the fence, but they were designed to assist the security force inside. They did not illuminate anything for the benefit of an outside observer. By now the meeting must be in progress in a soundproofed room. Dodson swore softly as he watched. Gradually he became aware that a helicopter was flying overhead. At first he thought nothing of it, but then realized that it was flying unusually low. He couldn't see it until it was nearly over the estate. Suddenly he realized that something important was happening.

"Harper six, this is Harper two, over."

Before the voice in the control van could answer, all the lights in the estate went out.

"This is Harper six, over."

The helicopter was directly over the house and hovering.

"This is Harper six. Come in, Harper two. Over."

In the helicopter Wagner looked down and saw three flaming signals forming a triangle around the mansion. When the power was cut, the three flames marked the exact location of the house. The aircraft descended with no lights to assist marksmen on the ground. At about one hundred feet altitude, a small beam of light from the chopper illuminated the roof of the house. The aircraft moved deliberately into position over a flat portion of the roof, the part that covered the dining room. Fifty feet below the helicopter hung the explosive device suspended from a cable. Less than a minute after the lights had gone out, the shaped charge touched the roof. The instant it touched, the demo man flipped a switch, and the charge detonated. Immediately Wagner began to reel in the cable, and the pilot gained altitude. Wagner felt a temporary sense of relief as they left the damaged mansion behind them. It would take only thirty-five minutes to return to the small airfield, where they would leave a second explosive charge in the helicopter to destroy any trace of their identities. They would have to wait considerably longer than that to find out the effect of their mission.

Dodson was looking at the house when the charge exploded. The sound was like nothing he had ever heard before. It took several seconds before he was able to collect his thoughts enough to respond to the radio message.

"Harper six, this is two. A chopper has just attacked the mansion. Over."

"I heard it," replied the voice, forgetting radio procedure. "What the hell is going on?"

"I don't know, but it looks like a hit. A big one."

"Stay where you are, two. I'll join you there. Out."

The detonation caused multiple reactions. The guards on the ground expected an attack and took up a defensive posture. The sedan drivers all ducked into their vehicles in order to gain whatever protection was immediately available. The

FBI agents felt justified in advancing to survey the damage. A confrontation was practically inevitable. Later no one was able to recall who fired first, but it hardly mattered. With the guards expecting an attack and the agents feeling that one had already taken place, there was an enormous amount of tension. Someone from either side could have fired the first shot. Within seconds, the estate was transformed into a battleground.

Dodson waited until his superior arrived, a man named Hyde, then both of them moved toward the entrance. On the way, they met an agent who had picked up one of the signal flares. It consisted of a tin can stuffed with cotton wadding and doused with gasoline.

"Paratroopers are taught to mark drop zones for a re-supply drop that way," commented Hyde.

Suddenly the lights came back on. Several of the security men were caught in the open. With no cover, they became easy targets for the federal agents.

With the security force thus reduced, the FBI men forced their way into the estate. All the frustration of the long waiting game had vanished with the turn of events. Now it was open season on the mobs, and each agent was determined to eliminate at least one of the gangsters while he had the chance. The lights now favored the attacking force, and none of the security force thought to look for the master switch to turn them off.

Dodson and Hyde reached the front gate just as the police chief from Lake Forest arrived. The latter looked utterly bewildered. The exclusive northern suburb usually avoided most of the unpleasantness of urban crime. The police in Lake Forest seldom had to perform any function more serious than stopping a speeding college student. Now they had a full-scale war on their hands.

"What the hell is happening?" asked the police chief.

"Somebody bombed the mansion from a helicopter," Hyde replied.

"Why in the world would anyone want to do a thing like that?" the chief asked.

"They didn't say," replied Hyde. Then he and Dodson ran forward, leaving the chief to ponder the situation by himself.

They had nearly reached the mansion without encountering any opposition when one of the guards saw them and fired wildly in their direction. The feds dropped to the ground and returned fire. Soon the shooting from that quarter stopped, and they continued toward the house. Dodson was amazed to notice that there were lights burning inside the house. He was not very anxious to go in and find out why. Apparently Hyde wasn't either, because the two of them just waited there for the action to stop. It took about ten more minutes. The last of the security guards, feeling isolated from the others, surrendered to the agents with no idea of the relative numbers involved in the battle.

It was only after they had been reinforced by several other agents that Dodson and Hyde attempted to enter the house. As soon as they went inside, three domestic members of the security force met them with their hands raised. Hyde forced them to lead the way to the meeting room. One of them said that the conference had been slated for the dining room. He led them to it, but the door was closed. Hyde tried to peek through the keyhole, but could see nothing. The windowless room was dark. The agents looked at each other apprehensively. They were about to open the door on one of the most distinguished groups of underworld figures that had ever assembled—assuming that they were still there.

Finally Hyde decided to exercise his authority. He took a deep breath and shouted, "This is the FBI. Come out of there with your hands where I can see them."

There was no response. Everyone outside the door looked

tense. Dodson reached for the doorknob while the others tried to prepare for something without knowing what it was. Dodson wrenched the door open and stepped back right away. There was no light in the room and no movement. It took a few moments for the agents' eyes to adjust so that they could comprehend what they saw. The shaped charge had hit the big crystal chandelier. The hundreds of pieces of cut glass had been converted instantly into projectiles. All the occupants of the room had been hit by many fragments of glass. The place looked like a slaughter house. Even some of the seasoned veterans felt queasy as they viewed the carnage in the dim light. Nobody went inside. It didn't occur to anyone to check for survivors.

Hyde turned and walked slowly toward the front door. The police chief was waiting outside.

"What happened in there?" he asked.

Hyde ignored him and walked on toward the front gate. He would have to report what had happened. That was his responsibility. But he didn't have to stay there and look at it. His responsibility didn't extend that far.

The helicopter carrying Wagner and the others reached the airfield from which it had departed. There was no control tower, and there were no personnel on the field that night. The pilot landed the chopper at the far end of the field. He and Wagner got out while the demolition man prepared an explosive charge and set it to go off in thirty minutes. Then the three of them walked back toward the parking lot in the dark.

"Do you think we got 'em?" asked the demo man, whose assumed name was Hughes.

"Hard to tell," said Wagner. "We hit our target, but there's no way of knowing if they were in there. And even if they were, there are just too many variables. We'll just have to wait and see."

"How soon do you think it will be on the news?"

"I wouldn't hold my breath. The FBI might restrict the area."

"Damn! I wish there were some way of finding out."

"What's the rush?" asked Wagner.

"Those bastards forced my father out of his business several years ago. He never got over it. He was bitter until his dying day."

"It sounds like you never got over it, either."

Hughes was silent for a moment. "No, I guess I didn't."

"Well," said Wagner, "If we didn't get them, I'll bet we sure ruined their party."

Hughes chuckled. "I imagine we did. But I'd give anything to find out how far that charge went down."

"If we hit that chandelier, it didn't have to go down any farther than that," said Wagner grimly.

As he drove back toward Chicago, Wagner recalled an earlier conversation with Sylvia. She had asked how he would recommend attacking the "untouchables" of organized crime, and he had responded rather flippantly, "You could rent an airplane and drop a bomb on their house, but that would be considered tacky in some circles." Tacky or not, they had just done it.

17

Wagner drove straight to Sylvia's apartment house. She opened the door to her apartment before he even rang the bell. Her sense of relief was so overwhelming that she didn't even try to conceal it. She simply threw her arms around him and held him without saying anything for a long time. Wagner had been too busy to consider how worried she might be. Finally she spoke.

"It's on the news already. The TV crews are going crazy trying to figure out what happened. They keep trying to interview the FBI agents, but they don't want to be filmed. Nobody wants to say anything about it. It's pure chaos out there."

"Yeah, I guess we messed things up a bit."

"I couldn't tell if you'd gotten away all right. It was pretty obvious that you'd gotten in, but I couldn't make any sense out of the report."

"I should have called you right away," he said. "I just didn't think of it."

"How did it go? Were you able to place the charge where you wanted it?"

"I think so. Let's watch the TV report and see if we can find out anything."

They sat down on the couch and watched the TV news reporters trying to piece together the various bits of information. The FBI agents looked almost comical as they tried to dodge the cameras. Finally the monitor switched back to the TV station, where a senior anchorman worked to summarize the developments.

"Ladies and gentlemen, the details of tonight's episode at Lake Forest are still sketchy, but here is the situation as nearly as we can reconstruct it. A top-level gangland meeting was taking place at the mansion of Paul J. Vickers, the recently murdered power broker. The meeting was being monitored by the FBI and other federal agencies, although they had no immediate cause to interfere. At approximately 10:15 the electric power was cut and a helicopter appeared, which apparently dropped a bomb on the part of the mansion where the meeting was being held. A firefight ensued between the federal agents and the mansion's security force. It is estimated that at least twenty people died, either from the bombing or from the ensuing battle.

"A spokesman for the federal government strongly denies that the helicopter was under the control of any of its agencies. He suggests that the attack came from a rival faction. Within the last twenty minutes, two groups have claimed responsibility for the attack. One is a South Side motorcycle gang. The other is a left-wing ecology group which is lobbying to have marijuana legalized and the eating of meat outlawed. Neither claim is being taken very seriously, however, since neither spokesman seemed to have a very clear idea of the location of Lake Forest. Meanwhile, our investigative reporters are busy trying to find out exactly what happened here tonight and why."

The station switched to a commercial break, and Sylvia turned the sound down.

"At least twenty dead," she said. "Did anyone expect so many?"

Wagner shrugged. "I doubt if anyone bothered to speculate on a body count. We just wanted to hit the conference room, and we had no idea how many would be in it. The shoot-out on the grounds was a bonus. We didn't count on that at all."

Sylvia shuddered. "I'm having a lot of confused thoughts

right now. I'm awfully relieved that you came through it all right. I feel a certain satisfaction that our plan worked. I'm scared when I think what might happen if anyone figures out what our part in this was."

"And you ask yourself if it was really necessary for all those people to die."

"Exactly."

"Well, if it's any comfort, that pretty well summarizes my feelings, too. It was a major blow to organized crime. Maybe the biggest ever. But I don't feel entirely satisfied with the outcome. I guess that's the catch to all this. No matter how successful we are, there's always the nagging realization that what we're doing is ethically questionable and illegal as hell."

She took a deep breath. "Maybe it's time for us to get out."

"That thought has crossed my mind more than once," he replied.

"We've already accomplished more than we ever dreamed possible. If we stay in, we're just waiting for the odds to catch up with us. We can't expect to get away with this indefinitely."

"Not when we're crossing the good guys as well as the bad guys."

The television news broadcast continued to report on the incident as more information became available. It concentrated on the battle which had taken place outside the mansion, but also made vague references to the bombing.

"The FBI must not be letting anyone inside yet," Wagner remarked. "They probably want to identify the bodies before they open the place up to the media."

Sylvia shuddered again. "I can't imagine why anyone would want to go in there."

They watched the news until it became apparent that nothing more was to be learned that night.

"I guess they've found out as much as they're going to for

a while," Wagner said. "I suppose I should go home and try to get some sleep."

"You don't have to, you know."

He smiled at her and touched her hair.

"Then I won't."

The next morning Wagner called in to the department and found Lieutenant Gerhardt in a very bad mood.

"Wagner, where the hell have you been? I've been trying all night to reach you."

"Sorry. My answering service didn't tell me."

"Cut the crap. Just get down here."

"Will do. Give me half an hour."

Gerhardt's mood hadn't improved by the time Wagner reached his office. The lieutenant motioned him to a chair.

"I'm too busy to play games this morning, so I'll give it to you straight. The commissioner received a tip that you were involved in that Fourth-of-July celebration at Lake Forest last night."

Before Wagner could reply, Gerhardt continued, "You don't have to say anything. You're not being charged. Frankly, most of us here think that whoever did it deserves a medal, but that's beside the point."

He paused for a moment as if to collect his thoughts.

"Here's the situation as I see it. I know that you've been involved in some kind of extra-curricular activity for some time. That bit of foolishness at the Marshall home came right after he got you in hot water. I'm pretty sure you had something to do with that. I don't know the full details, and believe me, I'm not looking for any. Whatever it is that you and your playmates are up to seems to be for the right reasons. But if I can figure it out, and somebody is making a phone call about it, then you stand to have your game exposed. That could be very embarrassing for the department, and it could be a lot worse for you."

Wagner nodded, but said nothing.

Gerhardt continued. "Frankly, I don't know where we stand on this matter. I doubt if the commissioner will require us to investigate on the basis of an anonymous phone call, but it's possible. I hope for your sake that you've covered your tracks."

Wagner declined to comment, but maintained an attentive expression as he listened to his superior's appraisal of the situation.

"We should know something about your status on the force by early next week. I'd like to have you back on duty. You're a good man, all things considered."

"I appreciate the vote of confidence," said Wagner. "I haven't had many of those lately."

Gerhard came as close to smiling as his dour countenance would permit. "You've had a rough time of it, haven't you?"

"I've seen better."

"Well, maybe we can get this mess all cleared up and get you back to work where you belong."

"I'm ready whenever you are," Wagner replied.

"Meanwhile, keep checking in, and I'll keep you posted."

"Will do."

Wagner left the building and walked across the parking lot to his car. He was just about to get in when he noticed that the left rear tire was flat. His first reaction was defensive, and he looked around warily. Then he felt rather silly for reacting that way. After all, he thought, the tires were three years old. Sometimes they go flat.

He changed the tire, stopped to get it repaired, and drove back to his apartment house. It was only eleven o'clock. Sylvia wouldn't be off work for another six hours. He didn't feel like doing anything in particular. He was aware of a let-down feeling in the aftermath of a big adventure. He had gotten himself psyched up for the raid, it had taken place, and then there was nothing left to absorb his remaining energy. For lack of anything constructive to do, he decided to run five miles along the lake shore, take a shower, then try to sleep.

An hour later he came back drenched with sweat. He took a long shower accompanied by Bach's <u>Brandenburg Concerto No. Four</u>, but then felt hungry rather than tired. He walked to a delicatessen and ordered a hot pastrami sandwich and a beer. By then he felt more relaxed, so he attended to some personal matters rather than take a nap. The afternoon passed in due course, and he went to Sylvia's apartment to meet her when she got home from work.

She pulled into the lot at 5:20, by which time he had been waiting for about two minutes. It occurred to him that each of them could practically set a watch by the other's schedule, once they had established a routine.

"Hello, good lookin'. What are you up to?" he said.

"Oh, I was just looking for some poor derelict to invite for supper. My good deed for the day. How about you?"

"Gosh, that's mighty thinkful of you."

"Is that anything like thoughtful?"

"Yes, but in the present tense."

She smiled and took his arm as they walked toward the building. As soon as they were inside the apartment, Wagner said, "Now you can tell me what's on your mind. They contacted you, didn't they?"

"Yes. How could you tell?"

"You had a preoccupied look on your face all the way up here. It was obvious that you had something to tell me, but wanted to wait for privacy."

"I can't keep many secrets from you, can I? That's what I get for getting myself involved with a policeman."

"I'd like to pick up on the involvement bit later, but right now why don't you fill me in on the news?"

"The judge wants to see you tomorrow."

"At his home?"

"Yes."

"Any indication of what he wants?"

"Not in so many words. I'd think he'd be pleased with your latest operation, though."

Wagner was aware that they were using cryptic terms to refer to their activities. Perhaps they instinctively feared electronic surveillance of some kind.

"I wonder if he ever realized how far we'd go with him and his scheme. He was mangling a pimp's Cadillac when I met him."

"As the ad says, 'You've come a long way, Baby!'"

"Haven't I now! Three months ago I'd never met you."

"And just look at what you've gotten yourself into since then," she teased.

"Nothing I can't get myself out of," he replied.

"Are you referring to the organization or my apartment?"

"Either one."

"Do you plan to leave before or after supper?"

"I'm hungry, so I'd better behave myself. At least for the time being."

"So much for me. What about the organization?" she asked, abruptly ending the banter.

"I've been thinking about that a lot. I think we were on the right track last night. We really have pushed our luck about as far as we dare. I got the same message today when I talked to Gerhardt. He knows I've been up to something, but he's trying hard not to find out just what it is."

"Will that foul things up for you on the force?"

"It might. I don't know yet.'

"What if you lose your job?"

Wagner grinned at that question. "I've been in the process of losing my job ever since I slugged that pimp. Maybe the judge will help me find something in another city like he promised."

Sylvia tensed up at that remark, but didn't say anything.

"Of course, that would depend on your plans," he continued. "It would be a shame to break up the act."

She smiled broadly, threw her arms around him and gave him a big kiss.

"I could probably be persuaded to tear myself away from here," she said.

"Good. And who knows? If we still get along after five or ten years, we might even consider getting married."

She resisted an impulse to hit him. Instead, she said sweetly, "I doubt it. By then I'm sure I'll have found somebody nicer than you. He might even have a steady job. And a real name."

He laughed. "Touché! Maybe the time has come for the masquerade to end."

"Actually it isn't all that important to me, but I'll feel funny writing to my friends that I'm moving away with Mr. X."

"All right. It's midnight at the ball. The handsome young couple has been dancing together all evening. The clock strikes midnight. The lady reveals her mask and reveals…"

"Mrs. Barry. That was my married name. But I took my maiden name back after the divorce."

"Which is…?"

"Sally York," she confessed.

"Sally York," he repeated. "Sally…Sal…My Gal Sal…Sally."

Finally he shook his head. "I'm sorry, but that won't do. It's Sylvia."

"Do I get the same right of approval on your name?"

"By all means. Nobody will know us where we're going anyway."

"I have to confess, though, that I already know your last name. My contact mentioned it. He assumed that I already knew. Now I know why you thought it was funny when I christened you Richard. Richard Wagner."

"It doesn't sound so obvious when you pronounce it that way, though. The composer, being German, pronounced it 'Vogner.' I suppose I could get used to being Richard Wagner."

"OK, what's your real first name?"

"You'll never believe it."

"Try me."

"You asked for it. It's Siegfried."

"I don't believe you."

"Why not? That's what the composer named his son."

"I know, but he was a German and didn't know any better."

"Careful there! I'm German, too, and we're easily offended."

"Is that really your name?"

"No."

"I didn't think so."

"It's Wolfgang."

"Are you going to play Rumpelstiltskin with me, or are you going to tell me your name?"

"Would you believe Michael H. Wagner?"

"What does the H stand for?"

"Hildebrand."

"Dammit, let me see your driver's license!"

"Why didn't you think of that in the first place?"

She looked at the card and read: "Michael Hans Wagner."

"I went by Hans as a kid. Neither the Army nor the police care much about first names, though. I doubt if Lieutenant Gerhardt even knows my first name."

"Do you know his?"

Wagner thought for a minute. "I'm sure it isn't 'Lieutenant.' Maybe it's 'Igor.'"

She frowned. "Remind me not to let you name any of our children."

"Oh, are we going to have some of those? In that case, maybe we should get married."

"You really know how to sweep a girl off her feet, don't you?"

"A woman," he corrected.

"Do you ever plan to quit clowning long enough to ask me properly?"

"Did you ever doubt that I would?"

"Not really. I know you find me irresistible."

"Even with your clothes on."

"You'd better. I keep them on most of the time."

He grinned. "Well, at least take off your apron."

She complied, but warned, "If you drop to your knees, I'll hit you with a skillet."

"No more clowning. Scout's honor. Now come here."

She walked toward him with a suspicious look.

"You know I wouldn't kid with you if you didn't return it so well. And I certainly wouldn't do it if I knew that it offended you in any way."

"I guess I started it as soon as we met, didn't I?" she replied.

"So you did. I think that humor is like music and other good things that bring out the positive side of our nature. I probably tend to overdo it sometimes, though. You'll have to tell me."

"I think there are probably worse faults than being too good-natured," she said.

He took her hand. "Your sense of humor is just one of the things I admire about you. You're fun to be with, even when the situation gets tense. You have a sense of purpose and dedication. I'm also vain enough to appreciate the way you reflect my own ideas and values. I've kidded you a lot about being sexy, but actually I valued you as a friend before I ever had any notion that we'd become more deeply involved with each other. That all developed gradually. It's there, though. I told you when you got hurt that I couldn't just walk away from you. Well, you're healthy now, and I still can't. I don't know where I'm going now, but I want you to come with me. I'm crazy about you, and I want to marry you."

She smiled, and her face became radiant. "Of course I'll marry you." She hugged him hard. "And I don't care where we go."

"I feel at somewhat of a loss for what to call you now," he said. "What would you like to be called?"

"Just take me with you, and you can call me 'Brunnhilde' for all I care."

18

The next morning Wagner called his office as usual. Lieutenant Gerhardt was out and had left no message. Wagner felt somewhat relieved. He was to see the judge that day, and he was afraid he would be called in again. Actually he was curious to find out why the judge wanted to see him. At the same time, he was ready to resign from the judge's shadowy organization and preferred to take his leave in person.

As he left the interstate and turned onto Highway 38 heading west, Wagner felt something akin to déjà vu. Less than three months ago he had made this same trip. In some ways, it seemed as if he had lived half his life in that time. He drove through Elmhurst, Villa Park, Lombard, Glen Ellyn, Wheaton, Winfield. He passed the National Accelerator Laboratory and West Chicago. Just before he reached Geneva, he turned off the highway toward the Carrol residence. The four-year-old Buick was parked in the same spot as before. The house still needed painting, but it was less obvious than before because most of it was covered by leafy trees and bushes. There was no precise appointment, so Wagner didn't bother to time his entrance. He rang the doorbell, and a butler came to the door.

"Yes, sir?" the butler asked.

"My name is Wagner. I believe the judge is expecting me."

"Please come in, Mr. Wagner. I'll tell him that you're here."

Wagner went inside and waited in the living room while the butler announced his arrival. As he looked around, he was not surprised to see that everything appeared just as it had three months earlier. At times he had felt as if he had imagined the entire encounter.

Soon the butler returned. "The judge will see you now. He has been quite ill and is confined to his bed. He insists on doing as much for himself as he can, though."

"I suppose he would," commented Wagner for no particular reason.

The butler led the way to the judge's bedroom, announced Wagner, and closed the door on the way out.

"Well, Mr. Wagner, we meet again," exclaimed the judge. He was propped up in bed but appeared to be feeling reasonably well.

"So we do," replied Wagner. "I really didn't expect to be called back here, considering the circumstances of our arrangement."

"Well, it seems that our game has run its course, at least for the time being. Your latest adventure has attracted more attention than we can well afford. But only because it was more successful than we could possibly have imagined. You know, we could have worked for years without achieving such a coup."

"I'm still not sure we got away with it. I know of two people for certain who suspect that I was somehow involved."

"Ah, yes. The police have been watching you for some time now."

"Then why didn't they try to stop me?"

"Why should they have? You were succeeding where they had failed repeatedly because of their legal restrictions. Why do you think they suspended you again? You were more effective outside their control."

"I thought the lawyer, Marshall, did that."

"So did he. Actually he just provided an excuse. His flimsy complaint would have been thrown out if anyone had cared to challenge it."

"So all the time I was worried about the police, they were on the sidelines cheering for me."

"Is that so surprising?"

Wagner shook his head. "I don't think anything surprises me anymore."

"The psychology of it all is quite fascinating. The police caught on to you because you were the one who carried out so much of the dirty work. They must have known that you were backed by someone else, but it was in their best interest not to try to find out who it was. They knew that if they exposed the whole operation, it would ruin our effectiveness."

"How about the FBI?"

"They were in much the same situation. But their position was complicated by the fact that the media credited them with the bombing of the mansion. That put them in a defensive posture and caused them to waste a lot of energy proving their non-involvement. That left them with fewer resources to devote to us. Actually, I really doubt if they care much about us either."

"That just leaves the mobs to be concerned about us."

"True. But they're rather lacking in investigative capacity. Some of them attribute the bombing to a rival faction. Others think it was an undercover FBI operation. Either way, they have no reason to suspect us."

"Lieutenant Gerhardt told me yesterday that somebody had mentioned my name to the commissioner. Do you have any idea who might have done that?"

"I presume that your lieutenant made it up in order to cause you to quit risking your neck. He happens to care about what happens to you. Probably more than you think."

Wagner shook his head and paused for a moment. "This has been one helluva bash, hasn't it?"

"That it has. And you only know part of it."

"In a way, it's a shame to disassemble the machine. It would be hard to reconstruct it, if you ever wanted to do that."

"I know, but that will be up to you or someone else. I'm getting to be too old for such things. I've paid for it with my health. I can assure you, you don't get much of a feeling of control when your main concern is whether or not you can move your bowels."

"Is your condition improving?"

"Yes, but my doctor won't let me do much. I'm to stay on a bland diet for two weeks, then we'll see where I go from there."

"I hope your recovery continues," said Wagner. "I think you deserve to enjoy your retirement."

"Thank you. It's hard to retire, though, when you've been active all your life."

"I imagine it would be. I found that unemployment got old in a hurry."

"I'm sure you would. You're the kind of man who makes things happen. Idleness wouldn't suit you at all. Actually it's because you made so many things happen for our organization that I asked to see you. I wanted to express my appreciation personally and offer a more tangible token of gratitude."

The judge reached for a box on his nightstand and rummaged through the contents until he found what he was looking for.

"Here we are," he exclaimed and handed Wagner a cashier's check. Wagner tried to read it without being too obvious, and found that easy to do. The amount was $5,000 in nice, round figures.

"That's quite a bonus," he said. "Thank you."

"Not at all," replied the judge. "The people who backed our ventures were extremely pleased with the results and were therefore inclined to be generous."

"Do you mind if I ask your advice about another matter?"

"Of course not."

"I'm rather uncertain about the advisability of staying in Chicago. I think I can get my job back, but I doubt if I can ever function the way I used to. What would you recommend?"

The judge smiled. "I anticipated that problem. It would not only be difficult for you to remain here, it could also be quite dangerous. You stepped on some pretty important toes, you know."

Wagner frowned. "You once mentioned helping me find a position somewhere else."

"That I did. Have you ever been to the state of Washington?"

"I was at Fort Lewis briefly when I was in the Army. That's all."

"I have connections that can get you a good position on the Seattle police force. How does that sound?"

"It sounds great. When could I start?"

"When would you like to start?"

Wagner thought for a minute. "In four weeks. That would give me time to tie up all the loose ends here, move to Seattle, and get settled."

"I'll notify my contact on the west coast. You should have your new contract within a week."

Wagner whistled softly. "You don't waste any time, do you?"

"Not usually. At least up to now. I expect to be wasting a good bit of time from now on, though. I have to slow down if I want to stay alive much longer. Maybe I'll take up golf. My friends have been recommending it for years."

"I never cared much for golf, but a lot of people do. There must be something to it."

"I plan to give it a try."

With that, the judge seemed to have said as much as he intended. Wagner contemplated for a moment the advisability of asking another question and finally decided to take advantage of the older man's agreeable mood.

"Sir, if I may ask, you mentioned at our last meeting a deep disillusionment with our judicial system. You said that you might some day explain to me how you came to get involved in all this. Would this be an appropriate time?"

The judge took a deep breath. "I suppose this would have to be the time if there is to be one, wouldn't it?"

Wagner remained silent, since the answer was obvious.

The judge leaned back and stared at the ceiling for a long time. Finally he spoke.

"It wasn't really any one case or incident that soured me on the system. No system is perfect, and I was hardly naïve enough to expect that ours would be an exception. But basically, I expected us to work toward the pursuit of justice. Too often that didn't happen. Legalism got in the way of justice. I saw too many cases in which a mockery of justice was perpetrated."

The judge reached for a glass of water and took a drink before continuing.

"I remember a young man who appeared before me after having killed his sister and left his mother paralyzed with a bullet imbedded in her spine. He claimed to be sixteen, and we could find no positive evidence of his age, although he looked older. He was removed from my jurisdiction and placed on probation as a juvenile. About a month later he stole a car and led the police on a high-speed chase. The race ended when he hit another car head-on. He survived the crash. The family of five in the other car was not so fortunate. After he recovered sufficiently, he was sent back to juvenile court.

"Then there was the man in Iowa whose farm house was repeatedly robbed while he was away. He called the sheriff's office, but they weren't able to stop the robber. Finally in desperation the man rigged a shotgun with a trip wire. The robber came back and tripped the wire. The gun fired and hit him in the legs. End of story? Not quite. The robber sued the farmer for damages and won. I just about hit the ceiling when I heard about that one.

"Here's another one just as bad. A woman in Arlington Heights decided to poison her husband. She didn't know how much of the poison to use, though, and he recovered after having his stomach pumped out. She was convicted of attempted murder and sent to prison. The husband filed for divorce. Then would you believe he was ordered to pay alimony? That's right. It was even upheld over an appeal."

Wagner reflected that the recitation so far sounded like a synopsis of the clippings which Sylvia had been collecting in her scrap book.

The judge continued. "Have you ever noticed how many Supreme Court decisions are divided 5-4 or 6-3? There we have nine of the top legal minds in the country, theoretically at least, and they can't come any closer than that to agreeing on many cases. I, for one, don't feel very comfortable with the knowledge that legal precedent is being decided on the basis of a 5-4 decision. I think that there are some serious questions being raised about the nature—or even existence—of legal expertise.

"Meanwhile half-way around the world the Soviets are sending people on Siberian vacations for political opposition, the Arabs are chopping hands off pick-pockets, and Iranians are executing just about anybody whom they don't happen to like very much. You'd think that between those two extremes there would be a happy medium somewhere. If there is, I don't know where. Most of the judicial systems in the world are either brutal or impotent. I don't advocate the former, but neither do I have much respect for the latter. And that's what we have here in America: a ridiculous, impotent system that coddles criminals."

Wagner had nothing to say for a while. Somehow he had expected the judge's reasons to be more personal. He could have matched those anecdotes with some from his own police experience.

Finally he said, "I suppose I should let you get some rest. I've been here for quite a while."

"Thank you for coming out here. I could almost say it's been a pleasure working with you, but maybe that would be just a touch inappropriate under the circumstances."

Wagner smiled. "I suppose it would, but thanks for the sentiment, anyway."

Judge Carrol held out his hand, and Wagner shook it. He noticed that the judge still had a firm handshake despite his illness.

Wagner left the house escorted by the butler. He started his car and headed back toward Chicago. The radio was playing something by Schumann, but Wagner hardly noticed it. He was thinking about how Sylvia would react to the news that they were moving to Seattle.

Epilog

As Wagner drove away, Judge Carrol and the butler stood at the window and watched.

"A fine young man," the judge remarked. "He served us well. He should have a bright future."

"Yes, sir," replied the butler as he took out a sheet of paper. "By the way, Beckwith wired from Miami while you were talking to Wagner. I decoded the message. He requests instructions for the distribution of the latest shipment from Columbia.'

The judge sighed wearily. "Tell him to use his own judgment. I haven't gotten used to the increase in volume now that so much of the competition is in disarray."

"Right, sir."

"What time is the detective from Evanston coming this evening?"

"Not until nine. We had to make sure that Wagner would be gone before he arrived."

"Of course. It wouldn't do for Mr. Wagner to meet his replacement, would it?"

"No, sir. It certainly wouldn't."

PART II

2005

1

Dean and Martha Heckman were driving home from grocery shopping. They were expecting company for several days and had stocked up accordingly. It was a sunny June morning in the Denver area, and the mountains were clearly visible without the customary smoggy haze. Dean and Martha had just celebrated their 40th wedding anniversary and were looking forward to semi-retirement. Dean was a slightly built man who had lost most of his hair before he was 35. Martha was a pleasant-looking woman with short hair which was still mostly light brown. Dean looked his 64 years; Martha could have passed for fifty.

"Tell me again about our guests," he said. "I don't want to seem too ignorant when they arrive."

"All right. Sally York was my roommate in college. She was very bright and interested in political and social issues. After graduation she started grad school at Georgetown University in D.C. There she met a congressional aide named Barry. They got married, and she dropped out of school. She stayed in touch with me, but she never let on that their marriage was in trouble. I was really surprised when a Christmas card came with only her name on it and a note saying that they were divorced.

"After that, she moved to Chicago to take a job. Somewhere along the line she hooked up with a cop named Hans Wagner. She was never very specific about how that came about. Maybe they'll tell us while they're here. Anyway, the next time I heard from her was when she sent me a wedding announcement. They were moving to Seattle. She never said why they made the switch. I guess the Seattle PD made him an offer he couldn't refuse. Here's another puzzle. When she married him, she not only changed her last name, she also changed her first name. She now goes by Sylvia Wagner. Odd, huh?"

Dean nodded non-committally.

"Hans stayed with the police force long enough to qualify for a pension, then retired. She worked with social services in some capacity. I forget just what. Social problems were always her main concern. She never had any kids of her own, but she always cared about other people's kids. Her father was a doctor, and he died while we were in college. Her mother died after they moved to Seattle. She was an only child and inherited a respectable amount of money. After Hans retired from the police force, they both went back to school and earned advanced degrees. Then they both taught at a community college somewhere in Washington State. She taught sociology, and he taught something related to law enforcement. They had their summers off and used the free time to travel a lot. They've been to Alaska several times. He likes to fish, and I think he got her hooked on it."

"Boo, hiss!" he replied with a grin which belied the apparent condemnation.

"Just checking to see if you're paying attention," she said. "So now they're both retired for good and seem to be enjoying it. I've invited them to visit us several times, and now they're finally coming. I'm not sure what to expect, but it's pretty remarkable that we've sustained a friendship for over forty years."

"I'd have to agree with that," he replied. "I lost track of all my university friends a long time ago."

By then they had reached their driveway, and Dean turned in.

◆ ❖ ◆

Meanwhile Hans and Sylvia Wagner were nearing the end of a two-day drive in their minivan. They had deliberately driven eastward across Montana in order to visit the Custer battlefield on the Little Bighorn, then headed south across Wyoming toward Denver. It was hardly the scenic route, but it avoided much of the heavy traffic found on most interstate highways. As they approached Denver amid heavier traffic, Hans remarked, "Run the résumé by me again, would you?"

"OK. Once more for the west coast audience. Martha was my roommate in college. Our backgrounds were different, and we took different classes, but we became really good friends. Where a lot of the girls in the dorm were more interested in the social swirl, we were both pretty serious about getting an education. Martha was very much aware that her parents had made a big sacrifice to send her to college, and she felt obligated to make the most of the opportunity. Learning wasn't always easy for her, and so she compensated by keeping her nose in the books most of the time. I don't recall her ever dating. Learning came easier for me, but I studied hard just because I found most of my courses really interesting. That didn't leave much time for anything else.

"After we graduated, I moved to D.C. for grad school. You know about that part. Martha went back to Omaha, where she came from, and lived with her parents while she started an administrative job at Creighton University. While she was there, she met Dean. He was some kind of a *Wunderkind* who had gotten into computers before they became trendy. He was a rather skinny young man with a receding hairline. She sent me pictures from time to time. Other people tended to write him off as a computer geek, but that was their loss. He was not only brilliant, but from all indications he was also very nice. It took him several weeks to get up the nerve to ask Martha for a date, but when he did, they hit it off right away. When the government offered him a job as an analyst in Denver, she agreed to go with him. They were married, and judging from her letters, neither of them has ever regretted it.

"He worked for the government for a long time, then started a consulting operation. People call him with computer problems after the more conventional sources have given up. Martha stayed home with their two children. Apparently they never needed a second income. She does a lot of volunteer work, though. About fifteen years ago, they experienced a real tragedy. Their son was killed in a traffic accident. They were devastated and tried to focus on their daughter. Her name is Louise. We'll probably meet her. She married an ambitious man named David Wade. He had his own construction company by the time he was thirty. They have two children, both boys. They live across town from her parents, so Martha and Dean get to see the grandkids often.

"That's about it in a nutshell. We're welcome to stay as long as we like. They have a guest room with a separate entrance. They've planned some excursions, like Estes Park, but their schedule is flexible."

Hans shrugged. "I'm just along for the ride. I have no idea what to expect."

"I'm hardly in a better position. I haven't seen Martha since college, and I've never met Dean."

"That's about to change," he said. "We're nearly there. Thornton is coming up in a few miles."

"My gosh! Look at all those little furry animals beside the highway."

"They're prairie dogs. They've taken over the north end of the city."

"I suppose they're a nuisance, but they're kinda cute."

Hans thought of a response, but decided to keep quiet.

♦ ❖ ♦

Half an hour later they pulled into the driveway of the Heckmans' home in suburban Thornton. The house looked like most of the others in the neighborhood. It was spacious without being particularly pretentious and was situated behind a lawn with a few shrubs, all having been well maintained. The garage door was open, revealing a small Buick and a minivan similar to theirs. The first impression was one of middle-class prosperity, but with no ostentatious display. Hans and Sylvia climbed out of their vehicle and stretched their legs, which were cramped from the long period of restriction. Suddenly the front door burst open and Martha came running out.

Standing in the doorway, Dean Heckman watched as his wife ran out to greet their guests. It occurred to him that "Sylvia" was the perfect name for the woman. Her hair looked silver rather than gray in the sunlight, and she wore it shoulder-length. In her seventh decade of life, she was still an attractive woman. Hans had also aged well. He still had a full head of hair, which he kept short, and his bearing was that of a man who had remained active all his life. Dean felt a slight twinge of jealousy as he realized that Hans was roughly his age, but looked several years younger. The thought passed quickly, though. He was not given to vain speculation.

The two women, obviously delighted to see each other after so many years, made the unnecessary introductions. Martha called her former roommate "Sally" twice, after which the latter said, "That's all right. You can still call me Sally. I don't care."

The Heckmans helped the Wagners bring their luggage in. Hans wisely remembered that he had brought some frozen salmon as a house gift. Then the two couples retired to the patio for drinks and further conversation. At first the two women chattered away in an attempt to bridge the past four decades. The men sipped their drinks and pretended to be interested in their spouses' conversation. The afternoon passed quickly, and

Dean started the grill to broil steaks for their supper. Martha had already made a big salad.

After supper, Dean excused himself to check his e-mail. He said that some of his clients required his attention on a fairly regular basis. He was gone for nearly an hour. Hans was tempted to ask him what kind of business was that urgent, but decided to let it pass. The two couples simply made light conversation until ten, then watched the late news on television and went to bed.

2

The next morning the Wagners awoke to bright sunshine. Their hosts were already up and had breakfast ready. After they had eaten and cleared the table, Martha proposed an itinerary for the day.

"I suggest that we take advantage of the smog-free atmosphere and drive up to Lookout Mountain. That's where Buffalo Bill Cody and his wife are buried. The view up there is spectacular. Then we can show you our city."

Hans replied, "That sounds interesting. I spent some time in Denver years ago, and I'm curious to see how much it has changed. As I recall, this part of the suburbs was still prairie back then."

"Right," commented Dean. "And our international airport was, too. It's only a few years old. The old one closer to town got to be too small for the demand, and there wasn't room to expand. Getting the new one up and running was quite an ordeal. There were all kinds of problems. But now it functions pretty well—except when the weather man acts up on us."

Martha added, "You'll see a lot of new development. When we moved here forty years ago, there wasn't much between here and Fort Collins. Now we have a sort of megapolis running down the eastern slope of the Rockies from Fort Collins to Colorado Springs."

"I suppose that accounts for the poorer quality of the air," Hans speculated. "I remember when the biggest problem with the air was that the elevation made it too thin for some people."

"It's improved somewhat. We don't notice it too much, but some people with respiratory problems south of us do. The population isn't likely to decrease any time soon, and so it will remain a hot item for the city and state government."

Dean interrupted, "—and on that profound note, I suggest that we all get in the minivan and go for a ride."

The four sight-seers continued with light conversation as they headed west to a two-lane road leading up the mountain. The conversation flowed easily, and all were able to participate. Even though their backgrounds and professional lives were very different, they still found that they shared many common interests. By the time they reached their destination all the awkwardness of their new relationship was gone. Any inclination for the Wagners to regard Dean as a technological misfit were gone. He could hold his own on a wide range of topics and never mentioned cyberspace unless asked.

The winding road up the mountain eventually delivered them to their goal. It only consisted of a small visitors' center and two graves surrounded by a protective iron fence. Buffalo Bill Cody had been the ultimate American showman of the 19th century, taking his wild west show even to Europe. He had picked this location, which afforded a breathtaking view of eastern Colorado, as the burial site for himself and his wife.

As the two couples looked off toward Kansas, Sylvia was reminded of a Barbra Streisand song and recited, "On a clear day, you can see forever."

Hans ruined the sentiment by quipping, "From Sears Tower in Chicago they say: 'On a clear day you can see about half a mile.'"

Dean and Martha chuckled as Sylvia feigned anger.

"So much for you, Mr. Aesthetic. Next time we'll leave you home."

Hans grinned mischievously. "No, you won't. You know you'd be lost without me."

"Right. The first half of my life was just a total vacuum, wasn't it, Martha? It never started until I met Mr. Wonderful here."

"Hey, leave me out of this," she said. "I've got my own Mr. Wonderful."

Dean smiled, secure in the knowledge that his wife wasn't just trying to be funny.

The trip through downtown Denver evoked mixed reactions. So much had been built since Hans's last visit to the city. Mile High Stadium and the new buildings were impressive. The seemingly endless road repair projects were not. Dean was careful to get back home before the rush-hour traffic started.

Martha had planned well and prepared a meal that only required reheating. They were all able to relax with a cool drink on the patio. Eventually Hans's curiosity got the better of him and he asked Dean about his profession. Just what was a computer consulting business?

Dean reflected for a moment, then asked, "How would you rate your computer skills?"

Hans shrugged and replied, "On a scale of one to ten, I'd say I'm about a two-minus. I've never needed to know much about them, and Sylvia could always help me when I got stuck. She's maybe a four or a five."

Martha commented proudly, "Dean is off the chart. He's the one the people with problems call when all else fails."

Dean seemed a little embarrassed by his wife's endorsement. He said, "You realize, of course, that the entire computer history isn't as old as we are. Computers were developed during World War II to direct artillery fire. I just happened to get involved with them when they were first becoming accessible to the public. I was even ahead of Bill Gates. But where he formed his own company and got enormously rich, I accepted an offer from the government to be a consultant. We moved to Denver because there was a regional office here. But before long, I was working from home and doing the same thing, although some travel was involved. Basically, I was responsible for setting up secure systems. The feds didn't want people hacking into government business. In the process of doing that, I learned how hackers operate and how to counter their efforts. As a fringe benefit, I can probably out-hack any hacker."

Hans exhaled audibly. "Somehow I can't picture you doing anything illegal."

Dean smiled. "I don't. If I did, I'd hardly be telling this to someone who was involved with law enforcement. I no longer work for the government, but I still do some consulting work for the feds as well as several big corporations which have similar concerns. Namely, I deal with attempts from outsiders to gain restricted information."

Sylvia joined the conversation. "Are you saying that you can thwart any hacker just by being a step ahead of him?"

"Not entirely. While working for the government, I gained access to some very restrictive databases. I was supposed to give them up after I left their employ, but I memorized what I needed to know. I never write the figures and codes down. If they were to fall into the wrong hands, it could be disastrous."

Hans asked, "Don't you feel a little uncomfortable telling us this?"

Dean replied, "Not especially. I haven't told you anything that isn't known by quite a few people. Besides, I feel that I can trust you. I consider myself to be a fairly good judge of character."

Hans continued, "Excuse me, but my police training causes me to wonder if someone couldn't force you to reveal what you know."

Dean smiled again. "I have several contingency plans for leading any such person down a blind alley. It would take him some time to find out that any information obtained under duress was fairly useless."

Sylvia said, "We could have used some of your expertise last month. Somebody found my credit card number on a store's file and made four purchases before we discovered it. The card company took the hit, but we had to cancel that card, and now we have to worry about what that does to our credit."

Dean shrugged. "Maybe it's not too late for me to help you. Let's go to my office."

He led them to a room at the back of the house and opened the door. The small office was filled with computer equipment, but it hardly looked like a sophisticated center. Hans reflected that James Bond's villains always had a more impressive display than that.

"Do you still have your old credit card?" Dean asked.

"No, I cut it up after it was cancelled."

"Do you have the new one?"

"Yes, I'll get it." She went back to their room and retrieved the card from her purse.

Dean glanced at it, and his fingers fairly flew across the keyboard. A few minutes later his printer started up. When it was finished, Dean held up the print-out.

"Does this look like your account for April?" he asked.

Sylvia looked it over. "Yes, but these four purchases were not mine. Somebody else used my account."

Dean went back to the keyboard without saying anything

and pounded out more data. About ten minutes later the printer spewed out another sheet. Dean read it carefully and handed it to Sylvia.

"Here's your alter-ego. His name is James Kling, and he's a 21-year-old student at U Cal at Irvine. He used your card number four times for mail-order purchases, where he wouldn't need the actual card. He probably used another number after that."

Sylvia was amazed. "Can't we report him now?"

Hans answered her question. "Two problems. One, he lives in a different state. Two, he only ran up a $941 tab. Law enforcement agencies can't afford to go after small fish like him."

"So what can we do, now that you've identified him? He'll probably go after someone else."

Dean answered, "With your permission, we'll employ the Dean Heckman method. I have his social security number and his account numbers for VISA, Mastercard, and AMOCO. I also know a spot on the Internet which specializes in just such information. If I post those numbers, Mr. Kling will be far too busy with his own concerns to bother anyone else."

Sylvia thought for a moment, then looked at Hans. He nodded.

"Do it," she said. "But I think your name should have been Hackman."

Dean pondered her comment, then replied, "Some guy in Hollywood already took that one."

3

The next day was another bright, clear one. The mountains were majestically visible. As Sylvia came out for breakfast, she quipped, "Three clear days in a row. We Seattle folks won't know how to handle this."

"I suppose it tends to spoil you," said Martha. "We see the sun at least part of the day more often than not."

Hans emerged from the bathroom singing, "And the skies are not cloudy all day. Home, home on the range—."

Sylvia interrupted him. "Now you see why he hasn't appeared on American Idol."

The Heckmans chuckled and invited their guests to sit down for breakfast.

After they had eaten and cleared the table, Dean asked, "How would you like to run up to Estes Park today? It's only a couple of hours away, and it's really something to see."

"Fine with us," Hans replied. "I was up there years ago, but Sylvia has never seen the park."

"I've heard about it," Sylvia added. "It sounds wonderful."

"It is," said Martha. "Better take along a jacket or a sweater, though. It might get chilly."

Two hours later they were approaching the last phase of their journey—the Big Thompson Canyon. The road followed the Big Thompson River through a narrow gorge for several miles.

Dean said, "I don't know if you ever heard about this, but there was a real disaster here maybe sixty years ago. There's a dam up by Estes Park with a reservoir behind it. A heavy rain caused the dam to fail, and all that water came rushing down the canyon. People downstream had nowhere to go, and a lot of them were swept away by the current. Quite a few were killed. I don't remember just how many."

Sylvia shuddered. "Nice of you to tell us that while we're driving up the canyon."

Dean looked a little chagrinned. "Don't worry. That was a fluke. Besides, they rebuilt the dam a lot stronger."

"Now I feel better," replied Sylvia. "But if it starts raining when we get ready to leave, I hope we can wait."

Dean reassured her, "We'll do that."

Estes Park was predictably full of tourists. However, the heavy commercialization of the area did not alter the fact that it is a beautiful work of nature. Located at the base of the mountains, it is surrounded by high foothills and covered with coniferous trees. Dean parked the minivan, and the four of them set out on a walking tour. Eventually their path led to the cable car, which took them up to the top of one of the highest foothills in the area. The view from the top encompassed most of the park and far beyond. For once Sylvia was speechless. She was the only one of the foursome who had never been there before, and she was awed by the grandeur of the panorama.

It was Martha who broke the silence. "We've been up here many times, but this view never ceases to amaze me. It's almost a religious experience."

Hans said, "I always liked John Denver. He wrote and sang "Rocky Mountain High" and even changed his name to

Denver from a name that only a German could love. When you see what we've seen the last couple of days, you can certainly understand his fascination with Colorado."

Dean said, "This is just the edge of the scenery. The Trail Ridge Road goes up over the mountains from here. That's quite a drive, and it's only free of snow for a few months of the year. It might not even be open yet. I didn't check."

"We'll file that away for future reference," said Hans. "We've driven all over the accessible parts of Alaska, but there aren't many roads that go up over the higher mountains. In fact, I can't think of any."

Eventually the four decided to go back down and look for something to eat. It was already late afternoon, and they hadn't stopped for lunch yet.

After they had eaten, Dean announced, "There is one more item on the agenda before we head home. I want to show you my pets."

Hans and Sylvia looked at each other, but neither had a clue as to what he meant by that.

Dean led them back to the minivan and drove just a short distance to the golf course, where a few golfers could be seen. "Now we wait for my pets," he said.

They didn't have to wait for long. As evening approached, a herd of elk started to appear on the edge of the golf course. Soon there were perhaps two dozen cows and calves on the grass. Then the lord and master appeared. It was a mature bull elk with a huge rack of antlers. He soon made it evident that he was in charge. As the herd approached the party of golfers, the bull decided to show them that they had invaded his turf, and he ran in their direction. The golfers gave ground quickly and fled. The bull seemed satisfied with that and returned to his harem.

"So those are your pets," said Sylvia.

Dean shrugged. "Some people keep dogs. Some prefer cats.

These are my pets. I don't have to feed them, clean up after them, or pay anything for them. I just come here and watch them."

"I can relate to that," said Hans. "We're gone too much to have house pets. We feed the birds. They won't starve if we're gone too long, and they do their business in the yard. I don't need a pet to meet me at the door and bring me my pipe and slippers. I have a wife who does that."

"In your dreams!" came the predictable reply.

They all laughed, and Dean suggested that they head for home.

Soon all four were engaged in lively conversation, but after an hour or so there was a lull in the discourse. It was Dean who broke the silence.

"Hans, since you're a former policeman, I'd be interested to know what you think of the Miranda law."

Sylvia cut in. "Oh, no! You'll be sorry you asked!"

Hans ignored her and responded, "I think that everyone should have the right to dance around with a basket of fruit on his or her head."

Dean started laughing, but Martha didn't get it. Dean explained, "Carmen Miranda. The Brazilian bombshell. She was a singer and dancer who appeared in several movies back in the forties and fifties. She was very small, but wore built-up shoes and outrageous costumes topped off with a turban of tropical fruit. She was very vivacious and seemed like a bundle of energy. It really came as a shock when she died of a heart attack while she was still fairly young."

"I apologize for my husband," said Sylvia. "You have to understand that he's a frustrated comedian who could never resist a straight line like that."

"Don't apologize," said Martha. "It gave me the opportunity to show that I'm not as old as the rest of you, because I don't remember movies from the forties."

"Right," said Dean. "And you were twelve when we got married."

"Time out!" intervened Hans. "You asked a serious question that deserves a serious answer. The Miranda law. When I was a boy, my parents taught me that ignorance of the law is no excuse. I grew up with that notion being somewhere up there with the Ten Commandments. Then came the ruling that suspects in a criminal investigation had to be informed of their right to remain silent, that they had the right to an attorney, that anything they said could be used against them in a court of law. If the arresting officer obtained any information without reciting the litany, the evidence could not be used in court. Ergo, ignorance of the law has become an excuse, and a lot of felons have walked because of it. So what do I think of the Miranda law? I think it's just one more way to make it difficult to get the bad guys off the street."

Dean was quiet for a moment as he thought about Hans's remarks. Then he said, "I'm inclined to agree with you. If someone is about to do something illegal, why wouldn't he find out what the consequences would be if he got caught?"

"Well, for one thing, most criminals are a lot less intelligent than you. But I still found it frustrating when so many of our laws dealt with individual rights that complicated our job of cleaning up the societal garbage."

"Then I take it that you are not a card-carrying member of the ACLU."

"No, and I'm guessing that you aren't either."

"Hey, guys, this is getting pretty heavy," said Martha. "Can we change the subject?"

"Your call, Hon. What would you like to talk about?"

"I think we should remember that Louise and the boys plan to drop by tomorrow. We'll need to plan around that."

"I'm anxious to meet your daughter and her family," said Sylvia. "You've been sending me pictures of her since she was a baby."

"She's thirty-two now, and her boys are five and seven. They live across town in Aurora. Her husband owns a construction company and is gone most of the time. We hardly ever see him. They have a beautiful home on a five-acre lot, but we don't go there very often. They always seem too busy to invite us, and we don't like to intrude. Louise sometimes comes by, either alone or with the boys, during the day. She doesn't work outside the home, but she has her hands full keeping up with that house and her boys."

"You don't seem very pleased with the arrangement," said Sylvia.

"Oh, I don't know. On the surface she seems to have everything. But something just doesn't seem right. Louise never complains, so maybe it's just my imagination."

By then they were back at the Heckmans' home.

4

The next morning the four ate breakfast, then Martha brought out some photo albums. The earlier albums contained many pictures of Louise and her older brother, who had died in a car accident. It was evident from their expressions that the pain of their loss had never completely gone away, but they were able to talk about him without showing outward signs of grief. Louise had been a pretty child and had matured into a striking young woman. She had attended the University of Colorado at Boulder and graduated with honors. Then she met her future husband, David Wade. He was a few years older than she and was in the process of acquiring a construction company. A hard working, ambitious young man, he seemed like a good prospect for a husband. One photo album contained their wedding pictures. The next several albums contained mainly pictures of the two little boys, Jeff and Mark. Martha seemed a little embarrassed to be showing so many "grandma" pictures and put some of the albums back.

Around mid-morning a silver Lincoln pulled into the driveway, and Louise and the boys emerged. Martha and Dean went out to meet them and hugged all three. Then they came into the house to meet the guests from Washington. Louise was still an attractive woman, but she seemed nervous, and her mannerisms were somewhat strained. The boys were polite and well mannered, but they seemed almost too quiet, more like miniature adults than small boys.

Hans hadn't had any preconceived notions about what to expect from Louise, and so he had no particular reaction to her. But when he looked at Sylvia, he noticed that she had a slight frown. She seemed to be picking up something that he was missing.

When Dean asked Louise a perfunctory question about her husband, she replied, "Oh, he's at work most of the time. Even weekends. He has a big project out by the airport, and he says he needs to be there to keep an eye on things."

No one asked any more about David. Hans had the impression that they didn't especially care what he was doing.

Martha asked Louise if she and the boys could stay for lunch. Louise said they could if it could be a little early. She had to leave before one in order to get the boys to their swimming lesson that afternoon.

During lunch Louise picked at her food and didn't say much except to respond to direct questions from her parents and their guests. The boys showed better appetites than their mother and cleaned their plates.

As Louise prepared to leave, Martha asked her, "Would it be all right if we stopped by your place some time tomorrow? You have such a lovely home. I'm sure the Wagners would like to see it."

Louise hesitated for a moment, then answered, "Yes, that would be fine. I'll fix lunch for you." Then she turned to Hans and Sylvia and said, "It's so nice to meet you. I've been hearing about you for as long as I can remember."

After they had left, Dean sat down and shook his head. "I'm worried about her. She's not eating properly, and she keeps losing weight. When we mention it, she just shrugs it off."

No one responded for a while, but then Sylvia broke the silence. "I'm afraid you have more cause for concern than just her eating habits."

"What do you mean?" asked Martha.

Sylvia mulled over her response, then said, "I've spent a

lot of time working in shelters for battered women. Victims of domestic abuse have a certain look about them. Louise has that look."

Dean looked crestfallen. Finally he said, "I've suspected for some time that something wasn't right, but Louise never confided in us, and I don't like to pry into other people's private affairs."

"But why would she keep it to herself?" asked Martha to no one in particular. "We've always been so close."

Sylvia replied, "Abusers tend to find some way to intimidate their victims. They usually threaten to do something unspeakable if the victim tells anyone. That's why it so often goes unreported."

Hans said, "Tell us a little about her husband."

Dean replied, "He's a big man. Played football in high school and college. Has a Type A personality. Seems driven to succeed in whatever he does. Money is important to him, and he likes to show off his prosperity. Built a big house. Drives expensive cars. I think he married Louise as a trophy wife who could play the charming hostess and give him good-looking children. He never warmed up to us much and seldom comes along when Louise and the boys visit us. I never cared for him much, but of course I never let on to Louise."

Martha added, "We were concerned that she didn't seem all that happy with him, but we never expected that he would abuse her."

Sylvia looked at Hans, and he nodded. "If you like, we can help," she said. "I think we need to have a heart-to-heart talk with her tomorrow and see what can be done. If you prefer, I'll try to talk to her alone. She might open up to me where she'd be embarrassed to confess to you."

Martha glanced at Dean, then said, "Give us some time to discuss it. This is a big decision."

"You do that," said Hans. "We'll go for a drive and come back later. Then we'll take you out to supper."

The next several hours passed in a much more somber mood than that of the preceding three days. It was mutually decided that Sylvia would try to talk to Louise alone, and then they would decide how to proceed based upon her reaction. Each of the four mentally rehearsed contingency plans, but no one voiced them.

They drove to Aurora the next morning and reached the Wade home around eleven. The house was an imposing structure set on five landscaped acres. It appeared that David Wade either had a lot of money or had borrowed heavily to create that impression.

Louise met them at the front door with a wan smile. She had applied some make-up to good advantage and therefore looked less stressed than she had the previous day. The boys came out to get their ritual hugs from their grandparents.

As promised, Louise conducted her guests on a tour of the house. It was as impressive on the inside as it was on the outside. There were five bedrooms, three bathrooms, a rec room, a den, and a three-car garage which housed a Lincoln and an MG as well as the absent work vehicle.

Hans whispered to Sylvia, "Talk about suburban overkill!"

She nudged him and motioned for him to be quiet.

After the tour, Louise led them to the dining room, where she had set the table for lunch. She had obviously gone to a deli that morning and bought an assortment of salads and cold meat items. If she was trying to make a good impression, she succeeded admirably.

When they had finished eating, Sylvia offered to help her

clear the table and clean up while the others went out onto the deck. The latter pretended to watch the boys playing below, but their minds were focused on what was going on in the kitchen. They only had to wait about forty minutes, but it seemed like an eternity.

As Louise and Sylvia joined the others, it was obvious that the former had been crying. Her make-up was smeared, and her eyes were red. "I was wondering how long it would take you to find out," she said.

Dean and Martha heaved a collective sigh of relief. They had gotten past the first step of reclaiming their daughter.

"Show them your back," said Sylvia.

Louise turned around, unbuttoned her blouse, and lowered it to reveal a red welt.

Dean erupted. "That bastard! I'll kill him!"

"Slow down," said Hans. "You don't want to go off half-cocked. We can do better than that."

Sylvia glanced at her husband and said, "Oh, no! I know that look, even after thirty years."

Hans smiled humorlessly. "We know what's been going on. What we don't know is what leverage he has. Why couldn't you tell anyone?"

Louise now seemed reconciled to putting her trust in these people whom she had just met. "He used me to take out his frustration with the rest of the world. He was careful only to hit me where it wouldn't show. He told me that if I ever told the police or went to a lawyer, he would disappear with the boys and I would never see them again. All I would have would be our debts, because he took out big loans in both our names."

Sylvia remarked, "This has a very familiar ring to it. Only the scale is unique. It was probably all a bluff, but he was pretty sure you wouldn't dare call it."

Martha asked, "Well, assuming that he's bluffing, why don't we just call the police and let the law handle it?"

Hans responded, "In the first place, it would just be her word against his. In the second place, she won't file a police report against him because it might not be a bluff. And either scenario is bad for the kids."

"Then what's left for us to do?" asked Martha.

"I think that Mr. Wade needs to be persuaded to change his ways," said Hans.

Sylvia threw up her hands. "Here we go again."

Hans continued, "I've been thinking up a plan which might solve the problem, but it will require all of your cooperation. The first step will be for Louise and the boys to pay a visit to Grandma and Grandpa again tomorrow evening. I want them out of the way when the fun starts. Next I'll need some rather personal information from Louise. Are you with me?"

The others looked around at each other. Then Louise replied, "What's the alternative?

5

The next day was spent in preparation for the night's activities. Hans drilled the others on the details meticulously, incorporating several bits of information gleaned from Louise. Among them was the important fact that her husband's project was behind schedule and the crew was working until dark. He therefore would not be eating supper at home.

Louise and the boys arrived around six. When Jeff complained that he was hungry, it occurred to them that no one had given any thought to supper, so they ordered delivery pizzas. Louise, following the plan, left a message for her husband on his answering machine. She told him that her car was acting up, and she would have to stay overnight with her parents, since she wouldn't be able to get it repaired until the next morning. Hans had assured her that it wasn't a lie. He had disabled the Lincoln and would reconnect the loose wire the next day.

At around nine, Louise put the boys to bed on a hide-a-bed in the basement rec room. The others had little expectation of getting any sleep that night. There were still about four hours to kill, and they used some of it to ask Louise insignificant details. Then for a time they just sat there, each lost in his or her own thoughts. Finally Hans asked a question just to break the silence.

"Dean, how did you happen to get into the computer business in the first place?"

Dean shrugged. "I always had a curious aptitude for numbers. For some reason, they just stick in my head. I could still tell you the serial number of my first bicycle. Where most kids learned in school that pi equals 3.14, I memorized the number out to about fifty places past the decimal. The same for the length of a solar year; 365¼ is a tad too high, which is why the Gregorian calendar was designed to correct the Julian. I could still give you the number out to at least fifty figures. Why? Just because I can."

Hans shook his head in amazement. "And now you have a bunch of access codes in your memory."

"It's really odd. I can just close my eyes and picture all kinds of numerical sequences. I review them periodically just to keep them focused."

"That's fascinating," said Sylvia. "I'm not sure I understand how it translates into your being a computer whiz, though."

"That's because you probably just use your PC or Mac to send e-mail or surf the Web. You can do that without being able to count past ten."

Sylvia replied, "Actually I use mine for a lot of my work—or I used to. But I probably didn't get involved with many figures beyond my checking account at the credit union."

Martha interrupted, "Would you believe that Dean could get into your account with just the information he has and transfer your money to another one?"

Sylvia looked shocked. "I'll take your word for it. I'm glad you're on our side, though."

Hans frowned. "Apparently you have access to a lot of personal information. Have you used it to check us out?"

Dean shook his head. "I never use it just to satisfy my own curiosity. I'm not an extremely religious man, but I do have a set of professional ethics which exclude the use of my unique ability to snoop on people. You probably have your secrets, just as we have ours. Let's leave it at that."

Sylvia had the last question. "How many people know about your capability?"

"Not many," was the reply. "And they're all on our side."
"I surely hope so," she replied.

Eventually the time arrived for the four to set out. It was one a.m., and the traffic had been reduced to a trickle. It took them about forty minutes of slow driving to reach the house in Aurora. Hans, Sylvia, and Dean got out a block away, and Martha drove the Buick to a point opposite a vacant lot, where she parked the vehicle and turned on her cell phone.

The three, all dressed in dark clothes and wearing caps, approached the front door. It occurred to Hans to be thankful that David Wade didn't like dogs. Dean reached above the doorway and secured the house key which Louise had told them would be there. He unlocked the front door, wiped the key off, and put it back above the doorway. Then they entered the house.

The street lamps provided just enough light for the intruders to see what they were doing. They had brought pen lights, but only planned to use them if absolutely necessary. Having just been on a tour of the house, they all knew the layout. The master bedroom was upstairs and to the left. They all moved cautiously up the stairs, realizing that if they were detected, they could be shot as burglars. Much to their relief, they heard the sound of soft snoring coming from the bedroom. The three tiptoed in and could just make out the form of a large man lying on his stomach on a king-sized bed, partially covered by a sheet. Hans crept to one side of him, Sylvia to the other. Carefully they slipped a cloth loop around each of his hands, then secured the other ends to the bed rails. Then he motioned for Sylvia to move back with Dean. "It's show time!" he thought.

With a hefty jerk, Hans pulled his end of the cord tight and hooked it to the bed rail. Then he pulled a piece of duct tape from his sleeve and slapped it across the mouth of the startled David Wade, who had been roused so unceremoniously from his sleep. The big man struggled violently against his restraints and made lalling noises into the duct tape. However, it soon became evident that he was caught face-down on his bed and was totally helpless.

Hans pulled the sheet down. He could see that Wade was wearing only the bottom part of his pajamas. He addressed the helpless man in a gravelly voice.

"Mr. Wade, do you remember the part of your wedding vow where it talks about loving and cherishing? Do you recall any part that mentions abusing and beating?"

Wade knew that he was in serious trouble and struggled vainly to get free.

Hans continued, "There are some of us, Mr. Wade, who have a pretty low opinion of men who hit women, especially when the hitter is much bigger than the hittee."

Hans suddenly realized that he was enjoying this too much and needed to get on with it. They didn't have all night.

"Mr. Wade, have you ever heard of caning?"

Wades muffled reaction indicated that he had.

"Well, Mr. Wade, you apparently have some familiarity with the Asian form of corporal punishment. Now, the judicial system over here considers that cruel and unusual punishment. But we're not part of the judicial system, and so we don't particularly care."

Wade was going wild trying to escape from his bonds.

Hans pulled Wade's pajama bottoms down, exposing his bare buttocks. Then he turned to Dean, who was holding a four-foot length of garden hose. Hans reached for the hose, but Dean, who had been cautioned to say nothing, shook his head. It became clear that he wanted to administer the punishment himself.

And so the brilliant little "computer geek" struck his much larger son-in-law thirty-nine times across the buttocks with all the strength he could muster. Hans kept count in order to make sure that Dean didn't inflict permanent damage, but then he had the absurd thought, "I think he can count to thirty-nine."

When Dean was finished, Wade was limp from the beating. Hans motioned for the others to head out. As soon as they were gone, Hans took the precaution of tying Wade's legs together with his pajama bottoms. Then he leaned over the beaten man and rasped, "If you ever lay a hand on your wife again, we'll be back. And we won't be so gentle next time." Then he unhooked the restraint on Wade's left side and moved out quickly. He wanted Wade to be able to free himself, but not soon enough to take any action against them.

As he ran outside, Martha was just pulling up on the side street away from the bedroom. Sylvia had called her as soon as they were finished inside.

There was a general feeling of relief as they drove away. Their plan had gone exactly as designed. Yet there was still that lingering feeling of doubt.

"Do you think he might call the police," Martha asked.

"I doubt it," said Hans. "Nothing was stolen or damaged—other than his tush. If he were to call the police to tell them that some people had broken into his house just to give him a spanking, that would raise some serious questions."

"Well, I just hope that we've accomplished something. We really appreciate your support in all of this," she said.

It was Sylvia who had the final word on the subject. "I expect that when Louise and the boys return home tomorrow—rather this morning—they'll find Wade complaining of a sore back and unable to work for a couple of days. He might suspect that Louise had something to do with our little adventure, but he won't pursue it. He might even gain a new respect for her. In any event, I seriously doubt if he'll ever hit her again."

"Wasn't that what this was all about?" asked Dean.

"Certainly," she replied. "But unless I miss my guess, it didn't give you nearly as much satisfaction to pound his butt as you thought it would."

Dean didn't answer.

6

It was nearly four a.m. when the two couples returned to the Heckman home. They found Louise anxiously waiting for them. Dean gave her a sketchy summary of the events, feeling rather embarrassed to be telling his daughter how he had just whaled the daylights out of her husband. But Louise showed more relief than any other emotion.

Soon they all retired for what was left of the night but, predictably, none of them was able to sleep. By six they were all in the kitchen drinking coffee. An hour later the two boys were up, and Martha started preparing breakfast while Hans went outside to repair his sabotage job on the Lincoln. In retrospect, he wasn't sure why he had bothered to disable the vehicle in the first place. Maybe it was just to spare Louise the guilty feelings of telling a lie. Still, he couldn't picture David Wade going out to check on it under the present circumstances.

After Louise and the boys had left, Dean went to check his e-mail and Martha busied herself in the kitchen. Hans and Sylvia realized that it would be pointless to attempt to engage them in conversation until they heard from their daughter.

It was nearly noon when the phone rang, and Martha answered before it could ring twice. The conversation was obviously one-sided, and it was fairly brief. When Martha hung up, she had three faces staring at her in anticipation.

"David was lying on his stomach in bed when she got home. He said he threw his back out. She offered to take him to a chiropractor, but he said it would just have to run its course. He'd had it before. She helped him stand up, but he can't sit down. He had already called his foreman from the phone by the bed and told him that he wouldn't be able to come to work. She just went along with his story and tried to appear sympathetic. That's about it. So far, so good."

"I'm sure he won't be giving anyone any grief for a while," said Hans. "The test will come after the pain goes away."

"At least he didn't seem suspicious that Louise had anything to do with the incident. It sounds as if she played the sympathetic wife role convincingly," Sylvia commented.

"She probably didn't have to act," said Martha. "Just seeing someone in pain would bring out her tender emotions. She's like that."

Hans frowned. "That makes it all the worse that he would hit her."

"Well, we've done all we can for now. We'll just have to see how this plays out. Meanwhile, would you two consider extending your visit for a while? We could really use your moral support."

Hans and Sylvia looked at each other and nodded. "There's no reason why we have to be back in Seattle right away," she said. "We can call the neighbors who are watching our house and tell them."

"We would really appreciate that," said Dean. "There's a lot to do around here in the summer. We can take some more side trips, maybe up to the mountains."

"Great," said Hans. "Meanwhile we can keep an eye on the invalid and see if he learned anything last night."

◆ ❖ ◆

Louise called them every day and stopped by once. David only stayed home from work for three days and insisted on going back to work as soon as he could bear to sit in his pick-up. When she stopped by, Louise already seemed less tense than before. Her appetite had also improved.

Sylvia mentioned that to Hans and commented, "I really hope this is a permanent change."

"So do I," he replied. "I'd hate to think that we went through that charade for nothing."

The two couples decided to make shorter excursions until they felt confident that Louise was safe. Since David was typically gone about ten or twelve hours a day, they still had ample time to go sight-seeing. Their first such trip was to Colorado Springs to visit the Air Force Academy. Hans and Sylvia were somewhat surprised to find it nestled in the foothills in a semi-scenic location.

"I had always pictured the buildings next to a mile-long runway," said Sylvia.

In anticipation of the throngs of tourists, someone had had the foresight to build a road all the way around the academy so that tourists could drive around it and see the entire campus without disrupting the activities within. Easily the most eye-catching structure there was the chapel, which had a rather controversial futuristic design.

"I always wondered if they designed that thing with some future notion of launching it into space," commented Martha.

"It certainly doesn't look anything like the cadet chapel at West Point," said Sylvia.

"None of it does," added Hans. "West Point looks almost medieval with all those stone buildings. It's hard to drive through the place, but you can't imagine anyone building a road around it. They'd have the Hudson River on one side and a pile of rocks on the other."

"West Point is about 150 years older than the Air Force Academy and looks it, but they're both impressive." All agreed.

"Have any of you been to Annapolis?" Dean asked.

None of them had, and so they had nothing to say about it.

◆ ❖ ◆

As they were driving back, another driver cut them off near an exit ramp. Dean gave vent to an unusual display of anger.

"You moron!" he yelled.

"Oh, please!" teased Sylvia. "He's merely navigationally challenged."

Dean's good mood was instantly restored, and he smiled.

"OK, Miss Political Correctness, then what am I?"

Sylvia thought for a moment, then said, "Well, since you've lost most of your hair, that makes you follically challenged."

Martha grinned and asked, "How about me?"

"Since you're a little shorter than average, that makes you vertically challenged—but not much."

Hans added, "—and since we're all over sixty, I suppose that makes us chronologically challenged."

"Yes, but we're also experientially enhanced."

They all had their first good laugh in days. Then Dean commented, "Until a few years ago, I'd never heard of political correctness. Had you?"

Sylvia replied, "No, because the term was just coined fairly recently. It's an odd sign of our times."

"What do you make of it?"

"We've discussed the phenomenon quite a bit, especially when we were teaching at a college. It might have been a by-product of the Civil Rights movement. It started with the notion that we shouldn't say anything that might be taken as offensive to anyone else. Score one for civility. But the problem with that idea is determining how far to go. By trying not to offend anyone, we lower the bar to the most thin-skinned person out there."

Hans added, "That includes the ultra-feminist who resents being called a lady because she considers it frivolous. It's also the 'person of color' who reacts against the use of 'niggardly' on the mistaken assumption that it derives from the dreaded 'n' word."

Sylvia picked it up again, "Quite a few college and university administrators have been sold on the idea that this is the fair way to go. Some have established speech codes. As a result, students have been punished, and faculty members have lost their jobs or been denied tenure for failure to comply with the new morality. One lesser form of correction has been to require people to attend sensitivity training sessions."

Dean shook his head. "When I was a university student, we were required to read a book by George Orwell entitled <u>1984</u>. It hardly seems so futuristic now, even if the title had been <u>2084</u>."

"This is where it gets interesting," said Hans. "Our friends in the ACLU have argued that our First Amendment rights permit us to express ourselves in any way short of libel and slander. So now we have one faction telling us to watch our mouths and another telling us that we are free to say whatever we want, within certain legal limits. It will be interesting to see how all of this plays out."

"Part of it already has," said Sylvia. "Consider the number of modified words which are now established in our language and don't seem to be going away any time soon. Stewardesses have become flight attendants. Hostesses are now hosts. Actresses have become actors. I suppose that if Grace Kelley were still alive, she'd be called an actor who became a prince."

Hans shuddered and grimaced, but his wife tried to ignore

him. She continued, "The feminist reaction to –man suffixes has led to chairperson, clergyperson, layperson, even waitperson."

"I'm waiting for woperson," Hans interrupted.

"Actually, there are some who spell 'women' with two y's."

"It's spelled funny anyway," said Hans.

"So are a lot of other words, but we're getting off the track. Think of our designations for non-Caucasians in this country."

"Where is Caucasia anyway?" Hans asked with mock innocence.

"Will you try to be serious for a few minutes?"

"I'll try. Go ahead."

"When did you first hear of anyone referred to as a Hispanic, Native American, Amerind, African-American, or person of color?"

Dean reflected. "You're right. But there's still a United Negro Fund, and the CP in NAACP stands for colored people, which has a more restrictive meaning than people of color."

"I take that to mean that we're in a period of transition. The situation doesn't show any sign of stabilizing just yet, does it?" judged Sylvia.

Martha spoke up for the first time. "Meanwhile we don't know how to refer to a lot of people without antagonizing them. Wonderful!"

Dean smiled at his wife. "You can just call me Hon, and I'll be happy."

On that note, they turned to less serious topics.

7

The next day dawned with the sun obscured by a cloudy sky. A light rain had begun to fall as the four met at the breakfast table.

"Maybe this is God's way of reminding us that we're getting spoiled," said Dean. "There's an Arab proverb that all sunshine makes a desert."

"The Arabs should know," said Hans.

"Actually we're not so far removed from a desert here," Dean continued. "Eastern Colorado only averages about six inches of rain a year. We've been in a drought mode for the past few years, so we shouldn't complain about a drizzle spoiling our fun."

Hans commented, "You know, it's really amazing when you think about the weather patterns. Just take the Pacific coast, where we live. From Alaska down through Washington and Oregon it rains a lot. Then it tapers off until you get to the Atacama Desert in northern Chile, where it hardly ever rains."

Dean added, "What amazes me is that we live on a planet which has a 70 percent surface of water, yet so little of it is usable that many people never have decent water to drink."

Martha frowned and said, "There would be more if we'd learn to take better care of it instead of fouling it up."

Dean concluded the discussion by saying, "Now would anyone care for some sanitized coffee and orange juice?"

♦ ❖ ♦

Since the weather was not conducive to outdoor activities, they decided to watch a DVD movie. They agreed on <u>The Fugitive</u> and watched it together. Then the two women wanted to watch <u>Fried Green Tomatoes</u>, but the men opted to pass on it.

"You watch your chick flick. I'll show Hans my inner sanctum," said Dean.

Dean led his guest back to his computer room and said, "I think I know you well enough to trust you with my personal project."

He turned on his computer and waited for it to warm up.

"Martha told you that I could locate your checking account and transfer all your money to another account. Of course, I wouldn't do that, but suppose I could transfer some ill-gotten gains into a charitable account, say a food shelf or the Salvation Army."

Hans whistled softly. "I'd say you'd better be damned sure you know what you're doing."

"I do. Part of the security lies in not being too greedy. I have access to the accounts of several big drug dealers and five groups that provide funds for terrorist organizations. The feds know about all of them, but they're being patient until they have all the necessary information."

"Have you considered transferring some of that money to the U.S. Treasury?"

"Yes, but a small amount, say under a thousand dollars, would hardly raise a ripple at either end of the transaction. If I knew when the feds planned to move in, I could make a bigger withdrawal, but I don't have access to that kind of information."

"Maybe we can work on that," said Hans vaguely.

"Meanwhile, a few hundred dollars sent to a small charity might spell the difference between someone eating supper or going hungry."

"Aren't you ever tempted to keep some of that money for yourself?"

Dean shook his head. "In the first place, that would make me a thief. Secondly, it would increase the chance of getting caught. And finally, I'm content with what I have. Bill Gates has made many times what I have and has been very generous with it, and that's fine with me. I don't begrudge him anything."

"I remember hearing that someone asked one of the old tycoons—J.P. Morgan or Getty, maybe—how much was enough. He replied, 'Just a little bit more.'"

Dean frowned and said, "I don't even understand that attitude. It must have something to do with power. Why else would a man want more money than he could ever spend?"

By then the computer had been ready for use for some time. Dean's fingers fairly flew over the keyboard. He paused briefly three times, then completed the transaction.

"That's all there is to it," he said. "Mr. Jorge Pensiero of Miami just donated $897 to the food shelf in Fargo, North Dakota. It's pocket change to him, so he might not even notice that it's missing. The people who volunteer at the food shelf in Fargo won't waste any time trying to figure out where it came from. Best of all, some hungry people will have food on their plates."

"How often do you do this?" asked Hans.

"Usually every other day. There are enough accounts that I only hit any given source once a month. I also spread it around enough that nobody is likely to write an article for the newspaper about a mysterious benefactor. It's all part of my security system."

"So you've become Robin Hood. You steal from the rich and give to the poor."

"Yes, but it's only the rich who are engaged in illegal activities. Drug dealers. Arms dealers who supply terrorists. Good folks like that."

Hans reflected for a moment, then said, "You know, I spent a whole career in law enforcement, but I never heard of anything like this."

Dean replied, "That's the way I want to keep it."

By early afternoon the drizzle had stopped, and the four went for a walk. The neighborhood consisted mainly of younger families, and that was clearly evident by the number of children out playing or riding bicycles. It appeared to be a safe neighborhood. Hans speculated that many of the neighbors would be greatly surprised, if not downright alarmed, if they knew what was going on at the Heckman home.

The afternoon passed quickly, and the two couples went inside to watch the evening news. As usual, the opening segment was devoted to the war in Iraq. Two more American soldiers had been killed by a roadside bomb that day. It was all depressingly familiar.

During the commercial break, from which they were mercifully spared by the mute button, Dean raised the question, "Hans, you served in the Army. What do you make of this business in Iraq and Afghanistan?"

"I served during the Cold War era, when our biggest worry was what Ivan was planning. This trouble with radical Islam wasn't even on the radar screen yet. I have my opinions about it, like everybody else, but I don't claim to have any profound insight."

"That's all right. I'd like to hear your opinion anyway."

Dean turned off the television news, which had switched to some Washington scandal.

Hans continued thoughtfully. "I have a friend who forwards

e-mail messages from his son in Iraq. He tells about reconstruction projects and community service efforts. Some of our troops are rebuilding schools and helping to restore electricity to homes. He describes positive relationships with the locals. Hardly any of this is reported by the media. All we get is the gloom and doom. Our opinions about the war effort are largely shaped by reports on what's going wrong over there."

Martha commented, "Isn't that what most of our news reporting is about? The front-page items are about who got killed or arrested. The less dramatic material gets buried in the back of the newspaper or at the end of the news broadcast, if it even makes it at all."

Sylvia added, "That isn't likely to change any time soon. The dramatic stuff is what drives the ratings, and the media are in a very competitive business."

"That's true," said Hans. "But the fact remains that our resolve as a nation is eroded by a constant barrage of negative reporting. It makes us question whether we're accomplishing anything over there."

Dean asked, "Do you think we're accomplishing enough to justify what it's costing us, both economically and in the lives of our young people?"

"In order to answer that adequately, we'd have to know what the consequences would be if we weren't there, and that's impossible to measure. 'What ifs' are always hypothetical."

"Do you think it's possible for us to make peace with the radical elements of the Muslim world by diplomatic means?" Dean asked.

"Not the way things stand now," Hans replied. "I have a theory about the relationship between Islam and what we might loosely call the Christian West. Christianity is roughly six hundred years older than Islam. Both set out to convert the world. Both claimed the authority of a text which proposed peace, but contained some violent elements. About six centuries ago, the Christian West, having tried to drive the so-called infidels out of the holy sites around Jerusalem without success, then turned to a systematic persecution of those who refused to accept the Church's dogma. Those people were called heretics, and the 'Holy Office' became better known as the Inquisition. It was the darkest page in the history of the Church. Now, some six centuries later, some elements of Islam are operating in the same mode. They proclaim that anyone who does not conform to their radical theology deserves to die."

"But they are killing each other," said Martha. "Sunnis are killing Shi'ites and vice versa."

"Consider the Thirty Years War back in the seventeenth century," said Hans. "Central Europe was decimated by the final phase of the Counter-Reformation. Protestants and Catholics killed each other over the right way to get into heaven. The real tragedy is that it didn't settle anything. More recently, look at Northern Ireland. That one finally seems to be winding down, but just think about how many Christians have killed each other in that mess. Even after they stopped burning heretics at the stake, Christians have wasted a lot of energy on each other. Just imagine what might have been accomplished if they had directed that energy in a positive direction."

"So you're saying that there are a lot of similarities between the dark sides of Christianity and Islam, some of it six centuries removed."

"Yes, but I wouldn't suggest that we carry it too far. Islam is a theocracy. We believe in the separation of church and state, but it wasn't always so. The Holy Roman Empire was founded as a synthesis of the two elements. Charlemagne was crowned emperor by the pope in the year 800. But for the next thousand years it was just a paper tiger, so to speak. Napoleon finally broke up the last remnant of it. But while the idea of a theocracy never really caught on in the Christian West, it is very much at the core of the Islamic structure. Muslims have never been able to centralize their faith other than through the Koran, but they see no distinction between Islamic law and civil law. That causes a huge problem when Muslims move to western countries and are expected to subordinate their faith to the laws of the new land. Some comply, but others remain hostile to the conventions of their new home. It's a big impediment to their assimilation. While some try to fit in, others remain an alien element in the host country."

After a reflective pause, Dean asked, "So where does that leave us with respect to a fifth of the world's population who are Muslim?"

Hans replied, "We shouldn't over-generalize about them any more than about any other large group of people. I'd guess that most of them are just trying to go about their business and don't give much thought to such matters. But focusing on the extremists who want to take over the world and kill anyone who is less radical than they are, I'd say that we have a long-term problem. We have a clash of cultures that defies solution or compromise. There has been a somewhat similar clash over here ever since some Europeans arrived with a radically different culture and confronted less culturally advanced people with no notion of property ownership. The two cultures were basically incompatible, and so the stronger one dominated. I think we're on the same path here. How do we reconcile a militant theocracy with a system advocating some form of democracy and governments based on separation of church and state? Some of the less militant Muslims have compromised in the interest of enjoying the benefits of a more prosperous system. Others have remained adamant in insisting upon radical fundamentalism. Those people are likely to remain a problem for us until the stronger faction dominates. That could mean that we're in for a long struggle."

Nobody had an immediate response to Hans's somber assessment. Finally Dean reacted.

"I wonder how many people realize how complex the problem is."

"Understanding of other cultures has never been our strong suit as a nation. America is so big and so remote from most of the world that we tend to marginalize much of the rest of it. That's part of the problem. After 9/11 many asked the question, 'Why do they hate us so much?' We had ignored all kinds of indications, and the few who had seen the signs were considered alarmists. Now they've gotten our attention. The big question is what we do with the information we have available."

Martha had the last word on the subject. "I'm sure glad that somebody wants to be president. I can't imagine anyone wanting to be in charge of this mess."

8

The next day was only partly cloudy. The two couples enjoyed a leisurely breakfast and read the morning newspaper. Martha wanted to wait for a call from Louise before planning their activities for the day. The anticipated call came at around nine. Martha took the call, but hung up after less than a minute.

"She wants to come here and talk to us," Martha said. "She sounds very upset."

All four of them felt a strong sense of shock and disappointment. Their elaborate scheme had seemed to be producing the desired results. So now what?

An hour later the Lincoln pulled into the driveway. Martha and Dean went out to meet their daughter and grandsons and did their best not to show any concern to the boys. They suggested that the two youngsters watch a video on the TV in the basement. If they suspected that anything was wrong, they gave no such indication.

After the children had been diverted to the basement, Louise sat down at the kitchen table. The four friends waited patiently for her to initiate the conversation.

"This morning I went grocery shopping while the boys were still in bed. I picked up a few items and went through the check-out line. When I ran my Discover card through the scanner, the display screen indicated that I didn't have enough credit to cover my purchases. I tried again and got the same message. So I switched to my VISA card. It showed the same thing. My cards were maxed out. I only had a few dollars in my billfold, so I had to take only what the cash would cover. I had to leave the rest of the items there. It couldn't have been a mistake. David must have maxed out our credit cards, and I have no idea why."

Dean put his hand on her shoulder and said, "I think it's time that we talk to him. You shouldn't have to confront him with this alone."

Louise sighed as if the weight of the world had been lifted from her shoulders.

"Thank you, Daddy," she said.

Martha acted upon impulse and said, "We always suspected that David was just too free-wheeling and inclined to live beyond his means. That's why, when each of the boys was born, we set up a college fund in their names. We also put just your name on some investments. We kept it a secret because we felt that if David found out, he would find a way to get his hands on your assets."

Louise nodded. "You remember that his parents died before we were married. He and his two sisters inherited their estate and divided the insurance money. He used his share to buy his construction business. He borrowed pretty heavily to pay for our house and all the trimmings. We've paid a small fortune in interest."

"Well, it sounds as if he's gotten himself in over his head," said Dean. "We'll just have to see if we can help pull him out. Tonight I want him to meet with us and our two financial advisors here."

Hans and Sylvia reacted with startled looks at each other.

Dean grinned. "I didn't say you were certified or licensed, did I?"

It was nearly nine p.m. when David Wade returned home

from yet another long day at work. As he pulled into the driveway, he was surprised to see his in-laws' Buick parked there. He went inside and found his wife, his in-laws, and a strange couple sitting at the dining room table. As usual, the boys were already in bed by the time he got home.

Louise got up and got him a beer out of the refrigerator. She handed it to him and said, "Sit down, David. We need to talk."

He was too taken aback to say anything and did as he was told.

"This morning when I went to the grocery store, I was both surprised and distressed to learn that you had maxed out our credit cards. I couldn't even pay for my groceries. Since you were already gone for the day, I went to my parents. I was too upset to stay home alone all day."

David's first reaction, predictably, was to become angry. He stood up and searched for words. Then suddenly he crumpled. He sat back down and buried his face in his hands.

"The Wagners are visiting my parents. They're from Seattle. They think they may be able to help us. It seems obvious that we could use some help."

David looked around and seemed to realize that he was no longer the lord and master of his own home. He had mismanaged his life to the brink of disaster. He looked like a broken man.

"I thought I was on top of the situation," he said softly. "I had some big bills, but I had money coming from three construction projects. When the first of the month came, I had payroll to meet and a stack of bills from my suppliers. But the customers who owed me money had excuses for delaying payment. It took all of my reserve to meet payroll, and I used the credit cards to pay the suppliers. The bank wouldn't lend me any more money because I've had trouble keeping up with my payments in the past. I'm probably headed for bankruptcy.

If I can't meet payroll at the end of this month, I'll be out of business."

Sylvia asked, "You have two very expensive cars in the garage. Can't you sell them and get by with something more affordable?"

David shook his head. "They're leased. If I can't make the payment on them next month, I'll lose them, too."

Hans asked the next question. "If you get the money you're owed, will that solve your problems?"

David nodded. "It will take care of the immediate problems. It's hard to say how long that would keep us solvent."

Dean had been scribbling some notes on a pad of paper. He seemed to be biding his time to make his pronouncement. First he asked, "How much would it take to get you out of this current mess?"

David didn't need to contemplate the answer. He had thought of little else lately. "Close to half a million."

Dean showed no reaction to that disclosure. He simply made another notation on his pad. Finally he spoke.

"I won't presume to lecture you. You already realize that you've been living well beyond your means on borrowed money. How you handle your finances is your business. But when my daughter can't pay for a sack of groceries, I get disturbed. I'm prepared to offer you a one-time bail-out. The credit card companies get about eighteen percent a year in interest. I will loan you enough to pay them off and cover your bills until you are paid for your projects. It's not interest-free. You can pay me five percent, which is about what I'll lose in the bargain."

David could hardly believe his ears. "Are you saying that you can come up with half a million just like that?"

"Did you think that I do consulting work for minimum wage?"

"But you live in a neighborhood where most people don't make $100,000 a year."

Dean shook his head. "You put a lot of stock in appearances. That's an expensive attitude. We have everything we want—except a happy daughter."

David looked stunned. "I don't know what to say."

"You don't need to say anything. Just think about it. Talk to me tomorrow."

With that, Dean motioned for the others to prepare to leave. As they headed out the door, David pulled him aside and asked him privately, "Did you hire somebody to beat me up the other night?"

Dean looked him straight in the eyes and said, "No, David. I did it myself. You remember that."

The younger man, who outweighed his father-in-law by nearly a hundred pounds, was absolutely stunned.

As they were driving home, Sylvia commented, "We've all heard the parable about the carrot and the stick, but it's usually in that order. Now we've seen it applied in reverse order."

No one had anything to add to that.

9

The next day David Wade took part of the morning off from work to compile a list of his debts. His estimate of half a million proved to be fairly accurate. Louise called her parents to tell them that he would be ready to meet with them that evening. Dean told her to have him come to their home to discuss the transaction. In addition to gaining a psychological advantage, it also gave them a reason to have the Wagners present.

It was after nine p.m. when David pulled his pick-up into their driveway. He had not bothered to change clothes from work and therefore looked rather disheveled and uncomfortable. If he found the presence of the Wagners inappropriate, he gave no such indication. Overall, he had the appearance of a desperate man who sensed that this was his only means of salvation from the financial mess he had created for himself.

Martha politely offered him a seat at the kitchen table and retrieved a pitcher of iced tea from the refrigerator. The others took their seats around the table. David produced a list of his financial obligations as well as a much shorter list of the sums which were owed him for work completed.

"I'm giving up the Lincoln and the MG at the end of the month," he said. "We'll make do with an economy car and the pick-up until we get this turned around."

The others were busy reading his figures and declined to respond immediately. After a while, Sylvia asked, "What is this figure from a Rocky Investment Company? It says that you owe them almost as much in interest as the principal."

David replied, "I couldn't get a loan from any bank last spring, and so I had to go to them. I was getting desperate."

"Twenty percent a month interest? That makes the credit card people look like philanthropists."

"Where I come from, that's known as loan sharking," said Hans. "Some call it usury. In any event, it's illegal."

"In some cases, it's known as staying afloat until you get paid," said David defensively.

Dean had waited to speak until he had read all of the figures. Then, having mentally crunched all the numbers, announced, "You will owe your employees and your creditors $502,407 and change by the end of the month and will owe considerably more if you wait very long to pay them. On the plus side, your customers owe you $541,087 if they ever get around to paying you. You could take them to court, but then you would have legal fees to add to your woes."

David said, "Our current project out by the airport will bring in $435,000 when it's finished, but we're a month away from completion. If we can hang on until it's done, we should be all right."

Martha asked, "Yes, but for how long?"

David didn't have an answer for that.

Finally Dean pronounced, "Here's my offer, which is non-negotiable. I will have my bank deposit $505,000 into your account as soon as you sign a promissory note. I will have my lawyer draw up an agreement that you repay $530,000 within the next two years. How you choose to deal with your personal affairs is your business, although I hope that you have learned something from this exercise."

Davis looked relieved, but he didn't say anything right away.

"Do we have a deal?" asked Dean.

"Only a fool would reject an offer like that," said David.

"Good. Then go home and get some sleep."

The big man mumbled something to the four and left.

After he had gone, Dean turned to Hans and asked, "What do you make of this loan shark outfit?"

"I would cheerfully turn them in to the police for violating usury laws."

Dean smiled his mischievous smile and said, "You do that. I just happen to have a hot line to the IRS. I can't imagine that a loan shark would be thrilled to have an IRS audit."

The next morning Dean set about the business of making good on his promise. He called Louise to obtain the Wades' bank account number. He could have found it on his own, but it was simpler just to ask for it. Then he made calls to his broker to sell some stock, his lawyer to have a legal promissory note drawn up and faxed to him, and his bank to arrange the transfer. By noon he had arranged all of the transactions without ever leaving his home.

Sylvia was amazed at how easily he could transfer such a large amount of money. "Won't your bank question a transfer of that size?" she asked.

"They'll double-check with me. They're pretty careful. I don't make a habit of moving that much money around."

"I wouldn't think so."

"But while we're on the subject of moving money around, I thought you might be interested in watching while I play my favorite game."

Martha frowned. "I get nervous when you do that."

Dean patted her on the shoulder. "Don't you worry, Hon. I know what I'm doing."

He led his guests to his computer room and turned the intricate machine on. While it was warming up, he told them, "I have the account numbers of four companies which channel funds to Islamic terrorist groups. Today we'll tap into the Atlantic Import Company of Bayonne, New Jersey."

"That doesn't sound very Islamic to me," said Martha.

"That's the idea," said Dean. "You probably won't see anyone who looks middle-eastern there either. But the import business is just a front for a set-up where sympathizers for folks like bin Laden can send their donations. The feds have been watching them for quite a while."

"Meanwhile you've been siphoning off some of their funds," said Sylvia.

"They're an easy target because they have to keep a double set of books. And they certainly won't call the police if they notice an odd withdrawal."

"And who will be the unwitting recipient of their charity today?" Hans asked.

Dean grinned mischievously. "How about the Jewish Anti-Defamation League?"

Hans and Sylvia burst out laughing. "You have a wonderful sense of irony," she said.

Martha wasn't laughing. She had heard it all before, and it worried her. It was only her confidence in her husband's competence that prevented her from saying anything.

Dean's fingers moved nimbly across the keys, and he was finished in less than a minute.

"That's all there is to it," he said. "$1,000 earmarked for al-Qaida just went to the Jewish Anti-Defamation League."

Hans looked pensive. "You know, I'm sure it gives you a big kick to play Robin Hood like this, but you have to limit it to fairly small amounts just to play it safe. But what if I could provide access information to major operations and still guarantee your safety?"

"What kind of operations are you talking about?" asked Dean.

Hans shrugged. "Use your imagination."

Dean thought for a moment. "The Mafia. The Columbian drug cartel. Darth Vader. How high would you want to go?"

"I don't know. Maybe if I just tell you what I know about the sub-culture that generates a lot of misery in the world, you can decide if you want to get more involved in this."

Dean looked at Martha, who was shaking her head. "I'd have to make sure that I wasn't putting my family at risk," he said.

"That goes without saying. I wouldn't do anything to endanger my family either."

Sylvia smiled at him, well aware that she was his family.

"OK, we'll talk about it," said Dean.

That afternoon the four sat on the Heckmans' patio and discussed the possibility of a future course of action. First Hans shared some of his experience with the narcotics trade.

"When I was with the Chicago PD, I was on a narcotics task force. We were dealing mostly with marijuana and crack cocaine then. We were just starting to hear about methamphetamine, which has become the drug of choice. But no matter which kind of poison we're dealing with, the distribution system is pretty much the same. It starts with someone who generates the product. Let's say it's some poor farmer in the Third World who can make more money growing opium poppies or marijuana plants than corn or soy beans. He probably has no clue about the lives he's about to ruin. Then somebody has to collect the crop and process it. Crack cocaine and meth require a chemistry set and some technicians. Marijuana is simpler to deal with. Next somebody has to smuggle the stuff past the Coast Guard and various other law enforcement agencies. They intercept some of it, but most gets through. Then you have a distribution system which looks a lot like that of a legitimate business. There are wholesalers and retailers. At the last phase of the operation are the pushers—the salesmen, so to speak. A lot of these are young men, some of them still in their teens, who drop out of school and have no higher ambition in life than to sell drugs. I had to deal with dozens of them. Typically they grow up in a housing project where unemployment is the norm. Their role models are the pimps and drug dealers because they have money and drive expensive cars. A young man who breaks into the business is assigned a specific area, maybe just a street corner. He deals with someone who is just slightly older and more experienced, who becomes his mentor. A juvenile has an advantage, because when he is arrested, as he most likely will be, he just gets probation. Jail time is just part of the cost of doing business for the older pushers. Sooner or later they will try to sell to an undercover cop and go to jail. Our prisons are full of people like that. But the prison system turns out to be a revolving door. It seldom makes a difference to a lot of them. They don't know anything else."

Martha shook her head. "This is really depressing," she said.

"It gets even worse," Hans continued. "Rival gangs get into turf wars. The youngster who has been given a designated area to work may find out that some other pusher has claimed the same corner. Drive-by shootings are not uncommon. Here's where the analogy with legitimate business ends. Ford may be in competition with Chevy and Toyota and even set up distribution centers next door to one, but they don't shoot each other."

"I would hope not," said Martha.

"The bottom line is that there are a lot of people out who are willing to risk being imprisoned or even murdered in exchange for a chance to make a lot of money. And if the truth were known, not very many of them make as much as they had expected."

Dean had been quiet up to that point, but he finally spoke up. "What I don't understand is why so many people are buying that stuff. Considering all the information about the effects of drugs, why would any sensible person want to try them? It's like using your brain as a tinker toy."

"I suppose for the same reason that some people deliberately get drunk. They're looking for some kind of a kick. I doubt if anyone expects to get hooked."

"Well, there must be a lot of scoff-laws out there buying it. If there weren't, most of the drug dealers would be out of business."

"That's why we've invested so much in information programs," said Sylvia. "We try to reach the kids before they're tempted to experiment."

"How successful is that?" asked Martha.

"It's hard to measure. How do you calculate why somebody didn't do something? Statistics show that we're making progress, but there is still a big market for illegal substances."

"OK, so what can we do about it?" asked Dean.

"That's the big question," said Hans. "Where most purchases are paid for by check or credit card these days, illegal ones are almost always covered by cash. You don't want your VISA bill to come with an entry that reads: six ounces of marijuana, $30, or whatever the going rate is. But since large amounts of cash draw attention, there has to be a subsidiary system for laundering it."

"Is that where the Cayman Islands come in?" asked Dean.

"That's one possibility," said Hans. "The idea is to find a place where a courier can take a large amount of cash without having to go through customs. It's also handy to have a bank with a 'don't ask, don't tell' policy."

"Didn't the Swiss banks have that reputation once?" asked Sylvia.

"Yes. They had numbered accounts with no names on them. But it became known that they had some accounts which belonged to the Nazis and others which belonged to their victims and couldn't be claimed. There were also allegations that various banana republic dictators and other unsavory characters were taking advantage of their system to hide their loot. It got to be too much of a scandal, and the Swiss had to clean up their act."

"And that opened a window of opportunity for certain small and independent financial institutions in the Caribbean," said Sylvia.

"They had a double advantage. They were closer to the U.S. and were exempt from federal regulations. I'd guess that there's a considerable amount of drug money deposited there."

Everyone was silent for a minute. Then Dean said, "I presume that you're suggesting that we might engage in some creative banking,"

Hans looked shocked. "Why would you think that?" he asked. "I was merely..."

"You're full of it, Hans," countered Sylvia.

Hans grinned. "You know I can only stay serious for so long."

"All right. What's your plan?" asked Dean.

"Well, since you asked, it occurs to me that we have to go back home one of these days to see if our house is still standing. While there, I might use my connections to gain some more specific information about the subject. Then we might continue this discussion."

"Fine. You're welcome to come back any time," said Dean.

Martha added, "We've really enjoyed your visit, even though it turned out a lot different than we'd planned."

"I can't believe this has all happened," said Sylvia. "We

waited forty years to renew our friendship, and just look what has come of it."

"It certainly has added some spice to retirement," said Dean.

"Well, we don't want to add more spice than we have to," said Hans. "It wouldn't be wise for us to communicate what we're up to by any electronic means. No phones. No e-mail. No fax. Oddly enough, the most secure means might be old-fashioned snail mail, but only if we can avoid specifics."

"How likely is it that anyone would spy on us?" asked Dean.

"Not very. But the best way to avoid problems is to assume the worst-case scenario. You've already stepped on some toes, and we're talking about stepping on some bigger ones. I'd rather err on the side of caution."

"I'll second that," said Martha.

"I have an idea," said Dean. "Why don't you fly out here next month, and we'll get tickets for the rodeo at Cheyenne Frontier Days. Then we can compare notes without having to worry about anyone bugging our conversations."

Hans and Sylvia looked at each other, and both nodded.

Dean continued, "Good. You tap your sources, and I'll talk to my former boss. He's rock-solid. I'd trust him with the key to Martha's chastity belt."

Everyone laughed, and Sylvia said, "I think you've been spending too much time with Hans. That sounds like something he'd say."

"I would not," said Hans with mock seriousness. "I didn't even know you owned a chastity belt."

10

Five weeks later United Flight 47 from Seattle landed at the Denver airport. Hans and Sylvia disembarked and walked to the baggage claim area, where they were met by Dean and Martha. They claimed their bags and headed for the parking lot. During the hour-long drive to Thornton, Dean and Martha filled them in on the latest news without even mentioning the main reason for the second trip.

"How are Louise and the boys?" asked Sylvia, deliberately excluding David.

"So far, so good," replied Martha. "Louise seems a lot calmer now. Looking at the boys, you'd never know that anything was ever wrong."

"Have you seen David at all?" asked Hans.

"Yes. They came over for dinner last Sunday. He was quiet most of the time, but he wasn't unfriendly. He was paid for one of his jobs and is nearly finished with the latest one. He also got a contract to build a motel somewhere south of here. He's still gone most of the time, but he does seem to be paying more attention to his family. It's a start."

"I think we sent him an important message," said Dean. "Somewhere along the line he got the notion that he was powerful enough to be able to do whatever he wanted, and there would be no consequences. Thanks to you, we were able to convince him otherwise. Now we can only hope that the better side of his nature kicks in. I don't think that he's essentially a bad person. He just got messed up by a series of reverses and reacted in a way that made everything worse."

Hans commented, "I guess I'm not too savvy, but I can't quite imagine why any man who has the least bit of self-esteem would ever hit a woman—unless she hit him first."

"You just answered your own question," said Sylvia. "Men who batter women nearly always have low self-esteem."

"How common is that?" asked Martha.

"It's impossible to know that," replied Sylvia. "Most women who are beaten are afraid to report it. I worked with battered women enough to know that it even happens in homes where you'd least expect it. Some men who are considered pillars of the community have their dark secrets. For others, it's a little like bullying in grade school. Some people pick on smaller people just because they can."

"I've heard that it occasionally happens the other way around," said Dean. "Some women actually abuse their husbands."

"Don't ever ask to see my back," said Hans.

"Yeah, you really look abused," said Martha.

"Seriously, it does happen, and the men involved usually keep quiet because they're ashamed to admit it," said Sylvia.

Dean shook his head. "I don't pretend to understand any of this. Most of us outgrow the notion of hitting people by the time we're seven."

"Well, you can chalk it up to arrested development," said Sylvia. "But some people are less civilized than you."

"Aren't you glad to hear that?" asked Dean, looking at Martha.

"I am," said Martha. "I have no idea about the statistics of all this, but both of us women have men in our lives who take good care of us and wouldn't even think of hurting us. I consider us fortunate. Maybe we shouldn't take it for granted."

Dean shrugged. "To me, that just seems the way it should be."

Hans added, "It works both ways. Our wives take good

care of us, too. Besides, if I stopped being nice to Sylvia, she might throw away the key to her chastity belt."

The Heckmans laughed, and Sylvia said, "I thought you said you didn't even know I owned one."

"I lied," answered Hans.

So went the conversation until they reached the Heckman home.

After supper on the patio, Martha put the dishes in the dishwasher, and the four of them settled down with glasses of brandy.

"Sorry I don't have proper snifters," said Dean.

"Why would you want a hunting dog anyway?" asked Hans.

They all chuckled. "It is a funny word, isn't it?" commented Martha.

"We have a lot of funny words," replied Sylvia. "Try looking up 'serendipity' in the dictionary. You won't find it."

"That's because your Funk and Wagnell is fifty years old," said Hans.

Eventually the conversation turned to more practical matters.

"We have tickets for the rodeo tomorrow, which is Friday. I've asked my old boss, Charlie Wilmore, to meet with us here Saturday. I've told him what we're up to in general terms, and he prefers not to know any more than he has to. But he's agreed to let us use the government's computer center downtown on Sunday, when everyone's off."

"Why did you arrange that?" asked Sylvia.

"First, because the system there is faster and more sophisticated than mine. Secondly, it gives us just one more level of security. If some hacker should trace our activities back to the source, at least it won't be our house."

"I'll drink to that," said Martha, raising her glass.

"So will I," said Sylvia. "What else have you been able to accomplish while we were away?"

"I've added a few names to my list and deleted two because they've gone out of business. I'm thinking of tapping all of them at once for big donations, then backing off until we can evaluate the situation."

Hans added, "I've used my contacts to locate some really big fish and where they do their banking. Since I don't have your memory for numbers, I've encoded the information we need, and I'll destroy it as soon as we're finished."

"That would be wise," said Dean. "We might get away with this once, but it would be a lot harder to do it again. Riskier, too."

"Then let's not even go there," said Martha.

"Fine. We all seem to be on the same page. Tomorrow we go to Cheyenne for Frontier Days. That should give us a plausible reason to be together again so soon. Besides, it should be fun. Saturday we meet with Charlie Wilmore and finalize details. Sunday we skip church to do some creative financing."

"It sorta gives new meaning to Super Sunday, doesn't it?" asked Hans.

"Let's hope so," replied Dean.

The next morning the two couples arose early, ate a quick breakfast, and headed north on Interstate 25 toward Cheyenne. Most of the early traffic was headed into Denver, but it was heavy enough in the north-bound lanes. It continued that way for about fifty miles, but after the Fort Collins exits, the traffic thinned out.

"This is where greater Denver ends," said Dean. "We'll see a lot of traffic in Cheyenne because of Frontier Days, but ordinarily it's a lot sparser up here. Wyoming has the smallest population of any state."

"I remember being there when I was a kid," said Hans. "We could drive fifty miles without seeing a gas station."

"Some of it is still that way," Dean responded. "But that has its advantages. We should start seeing antelope as we approach Wyoming."

"We saw quite a few on the way down last month," said Sylvia.

"They're really unique animals," said Dean as they passed the first small herd. "They aren't really antelope, and they have no living relatives anywhere. Technically, they're pronghorns, and they're the fastest land animal in North America. They can run sixty miles an hour."

"I've heard that an antelope—or pronghorn—two hours old can outrun a racehorse," said Hans.

"Isn't that amazing? Whatever nature is, it takes care of them. They're born right out in the open, where there's no place to hide. If they couldn't get up and move right away, they'd be lunch for some predator."

"Look! There's a whole herd of them," exclaimed Martha.

They continued to watch antelope all the way to Cheyenne, but just across the Wyoming border Dean said, "If you look to your right, you might see some buffalo. The Terry Ranch has a herd."

Sylvia said, "I don't see any buffalo, but unless I'm mistaken, that's a camel over there."

"Well, that just shows to go ya," said Dean with a fake western drawl. "You never know what to expect out here."

◆ ❖ ◆

A few minutes later they arrived in Cheyenne. Dean knew when the parade would be starting and where there would be available parking. He parked on the south side of the city, and the four carried their blankets across the viaduct to a grassy spot near the old Union Pacific Railroad station. There they waited until the parade started in late morning. The sides of the street were lined with crowds, most of them attired in western fashion. Police on motorcycles drove by at intervals to make sure that the parade route was kept clear.

Eventually the parade came by their vantage point. It began with people on horseback carrying flags. Then for the next hour and more came high school bands, more horses, floats, horse-drawn carriages, people in 19th-century costume, the Budweiser wagon drawn by Clydesdale horses, vehicles to wash down and clean up what the horses had deposited, Indians from a reservation in South Dakota, cowboy bands on flat beds, a caged buffalo, the simulated hanging of a cattle rustler, cowboys supposedly branding calves, more horses, Shriners in mini-cars, people on old bicycles, antique vehicles, and more bands. Then, just as the parade ended, a flight of Air Force precision jets flew over in tight formation to add a punctuation mark to the spectacle.

"Wow! You couldn't do much better than that for free entertainment," remarked Sylvia.

"We thought you'd enjoy it," said Martha.

They walked back over the viaduct to the minivan, then drove around the west edge of town to the rodeo grounds. They found a place to park in the huge parking lot, and Dean retrieved a large picnic cooler from the back of the vehicle.

"There's no point in fighting the crowds for lunch," he said. Martha had made sandwiches and packed a variety of canned beverages. By the time the four had finished eating, they still had an hour before the rodeo started. They walked to the grandstands, visited the rest rooms, and found their reserved seats. Just before the rodeo started, the announcer informed the audience that all fifty states and several foreign countries were represented in the parking lot.

Sylvia was the only one of the four who had never seen a rodeo before, and so she had no basis for comparison for the claim "The granddaddy of 'em all." It was the oldest rodeo, and only the Calgary Stampede could rival it in magnitude. For most of the afternoon they watched some of the best riders, ropers, steer wrestlers, and western showmen in the world. The spectacle ended with the wild horse race, in which teams of four cowboys attempted to saddle a wild horse and have one of them ride it around the track. As was often the case, some of the teams didn't even succeed in getting the saddle on the horse, while some got it saddled and mounted, only to have the horse run the wrong way. It took both skill and luck for anyone to finish the race, let alone win. It provided a wild finale for a wild show.

As they were walking back to the car, Sylvia told Hans, "Well, now that you're retired, here's a possibility for a new hobby."

"Yeah, I thought I might take up bull riding. It looks like it would be a lot of fun."

"Right. And I'll take up sky diving."

"You go right ahead," said Dean. "I think I'll take up chess—or maybe stamp collecting."

"I'm disappointed in you," said Martha. "I was going to buy you a motorcycle for Christmas."

"Only if you ride on the back," he replied.

They decided to pass on the carnival rides and headed back toward Denver.

11

The next day was Saturday, or D-Day minus one. They were all up well before seven, but it didn't occur to any of them to notice what the weather was like. This was their day to decide just how to proceed with their plan. High on their priority list were which targets to attack, how much to withdraw, where to divert the money, and what the sequence of events should be.

Charlie Wilmore arrived around mid-morning. He was a round-faced man, slightly overweight, probably a little older than Hans and Dean. If he was uncomfortable with their scheme, he didn't show it. Ostensibly, his primary function in the plot was to unlock the door to the building which housed the computer room and show them how to lock up after they were finished.

After Hans and Sylvia had met him and talked to him for a while, they sensed a kindred spirit. He had said that he didn't want to know exactly what they were doing, but the more he learned about the project, the more he seemed intrigued by it. He had known about Dean's activities for some time, and gradually he had lost some of his bureaucratic sense of propriety in the matter.

"I've known for a long time that you've been hacking in on some nasty folks and redistributing their wealth, but I'd like to know where your friends fit into the picture. After all, I'm sticking my neck out to help you do whatever it is you're doing."

Dean fielded the question. "Hans is a former law

enforcement officer from Seattle and Chicago before that. He has access to a considerable amount of information regarding organized crime and terrorist cells. Sylvia is a sociologist who has provided a lot of supplementary data. They add a much larger dimension to what I've been doing. I've only been able to be an irritant to middle-weight contenders. They can enable me to put a major hurt on some of the heavy-weights."

Charlie mulled that over for a minute. Hans speculated that he hadn't achieved his position by being the least bit inept.

"If I'm hearing what I think I'm hearing, you might be on the verge of doing something really important. Would you trust me to fill me in a little more?"

Dean looked at Martha and grinned.

"Don't you dare tell him that!" she exclaimed.

"Tell me what?" asked Charlie.

"It's a private joke. Never mind. The answer to your question is that I trust you enough to tell you that we're planning to make some serious transfers of capital tomorrow, none of which will go to us."

"Then where will it go?" asked Charlie.

"Most of it will go to the U.S. Treasury. It might even pay for a couple of days of our adventure in Iraq. We're still working out the details for the beneficiaries. But the main thrust of this isn't who will benefit, but rather who will be deprived and what they might do about it."

Charlie whistled softly. "I hadn't thought of that."

"Maybe you'll want to. We're still open to suggestions."

After a few moments, Charlie asked, "Could I stay for the party tomorrow? This could cause all of us a lot of trouble, but we'll never have another opportunity like this."

Dean replied, "I hadn't even thought about who would be there tomorrow other than Hans and I. Who else wants to come?"

"I wouldn't miss it for the world," said Sylvia.

Martha sighed. "I'll pack lunch."

The next morning the four were on their way to downtown Denver by seven. The contrast between Sunday morning traffic and that of a weekday was striking, even if it was predictable. They pulled into the private parking lot of a nondescript building and found that Charlie was already there. He held the door open for them with just a nod.

The five conspirators walked down a hallway to the computer room. It was a stark-looking enclosure with no windows and housed a state-of-the-art array of machines. Charlie had already turned them on.

"Do you have any idea how long this will take?" asked Martha.

"It just depends on how long it will take me to get in," replied Dean. "So the short answer is 'no.'"

Dean sat down and turned to Charlie. "Our game plan is to alternate the difficult ones with the easy ones. That's to keep my brain from overheating."

" "I can't even pour beer on his head. He says no beer until he's done," said Hans.

"This will take all my concentration," said Dean. "Martha made some iced tea for me. The rest of you can drink whatever you like."

Hans acted as moderator for the others. "Now, for our first project, we will target a California syndicate which specializes in drugs imported from Mexico and points south. They have generously distributed their earnings over three financial institutions in Los Angeles, Bakersfield, and Pomona. Some of my former colleagues were helpful enough to provide some useful account numbers."

Dean's flying fingers did their magic and located the accounts.

"This time we have agreed to enhance the California state treasury, since it has taken quite a beating from these folks."

Within minutes, Dean had made the transfers.

"A few million here, a few million there, pretty soon we're talking about real money," Hans paraphrased.

"Next we move to our friends in Bayonne, New Jersey, who have been gathering contributions for al Qaida. The U.S. Treasury gets five million of their funds.

"Now look under N for Nevada. Some folks in organized crime have been skimming off a lot of that loose casino cash to pay for drug shipments from Asia. They bank in San Diego. Ten million should pay for a lot of drug rehabilitation.

"As for our friend, Jorge Pensiero in Miami, he's fallen on hard times. How about just a million for the Salvation Army?"

And so it went for the next three hours. Then Hans announced, "Finally, boys and girls, the event you've all been waiting for: The Cayman Islands. Here we have located six banks which play the 'don't ask, don't tell' game. Private planes fly there daily to deposit cash from drug sales. The Russian Mafia banks there. It's trickier to transfer money from these banks, because it gets into international problems. And so, boys and girls, we're going to show you a magic trick. We're going to make fifty-nine bank accounts disappear. Now just use your imaginations. Picture some Mafia don or petty dictator trying to deal with a bank statement which shows a goose egg for his megabucks account." He shook his head. "Not a pretty picture."

The process took another two hours. When Dean turned off the computers, he was drenched in sweat and looked as if he had just run a marathon. Martha looked at him and threw her arms around him. He said, "If you don't mind, I'll have that beer now."

` Charlie came up to him and said, "The hardest part about this for me is that I won't be able to tell anyone about it. I don't care what the consequences of this may be, it was worth it."

As they were walking back to the car, Martha asked, "Just for the record, how much money do you suppose you moved today?"

Dean looked at her and said, "Eight billion, seven hundred million, four hundred fifty thousand dollars in dirty money."

Martha looked at him and smiled proudly, "I love it when you talk dirty."

Epilog

Several weeks later Hans and Sylvia were home watching the evening news, where reports of hurricanes on the other side of the country dominated the broadcast. The telephone rang, and Sylvia went into the other room to answer it. When she returned a few minutes later, her face was pale, and she looked shocked.

"What's wrong?" asked Hans.

"It was Martha. Dean has had a stroke."

Hans turned off the news. "How serious was it?" was the obvious question.

"It wasn't too severe," she replied. "He's expected to make a full recovery. But all the numbers. They're gone. He can't even remember his address."

Printed in the United States
213162BV00008B/4/P